PHANTOM HOLLOW

When Tony Frost and his colleague
Jack Denton arrive for a holiday at
Monk's Lodge, an ancient cottage
deep in the Somerset countryside,
they are immediately warned off by
the local villagers and a message
scrawled in crimson across a windowpane: 'THERE IS DANGER. GO
WHILE YOU CAN!' Tony invites his
friend, the famous dramatist and
criminologist Trevor Lowe, to come
and help — but the investigation
takes a sinister turn when the dead
body of a missing estate agent is found
behind a locked door in the cottage . . .

GERALD VERNER

PHANTOM HOLLOW

Complete and Unabridged

LINFORD
Leicester

First published in Great Britain

First Linford Edition
published 2017

A catalogue record for this book is available
from the British Library.

ISBN 978–1–4448–3205–1

Published by
F. A. Thorpe (Publishing)
Anstey, Leicestershire

Set by Words & Graphics Ltd.
Anstey, Leicestershire
Printed and bound in Great Britain by
T. J. International Ltd., Padstow, Cornwall

This book is printed on acid-free paper

TO MRS. EDGAR WALLACE

1

The Crimson Warning

Tony Frost gazed admiringly at an old Jacobean carved chest. 'That would fetch quids in a sale room, Jack, old boy, literally quids! And the whole place is simply teeming with this stuff, absolutely full of it, upstairs as well!'

Jack Denton grinned. 'Tony, you deserve a wreath of laurels for digging out this wonderful spot,' he said enthusiastically.

'By Jove, I really believe I do, you know!' agreed Tony modestly. 'The agent chappie said the same thing when he handed over the keys. He said there wasn't another cottage in the whole of England to touch Monk's Lodge at the rental, and that I certainly knew what I was about when I approached him.'

Jack Denton ran his eyes approvingly along the rough oak beams supporting the ceiling. 'It all looks fine,' he remarked. 'Let's see what it's like upstairs.'

Tony led the way out to the tiny hall, and the contrast between the two men was very marked. Jack Denton, though not as tall as his friend, was of an athletic build, with good-looking, clear-cut features, and wavy brown hair that grew well off his forehead. Tony, on the other hand, was inclined to be rather a weedy specimen, with narrow shoulders and a pimple of a chin that threatened to become part of his neck. His hair, which he wore well plastered down, had the appearance of a close-fitting cap of honey-coloured satin. His eyes were of a pale blue that gave him an extraordinarily washed-out appearance, and he spoke with a slight impediment of his speech that was more than a stammer and yet not quite a stutter. Combined with his fastidious style of dressing, these characteristics gave most people the impression that he was rather inane. Actually, however, Tony was not such a fool as he looked — and this is saying a great deal.

Like many other friendships, theirs had started at school, but unlike the majority had been kept up in after-life. They had gone up to Oxford together, but Jack, who had originally intended to be an engineer, had been compelled to leave before he had completed his time, owing to the death of his father, which resulted in certain drastic alterations to his financial expectations. So drastic indeed were these alterations that his original career as an engineer had to be abandoned, and he had been forced to take the first job that had come along.

Tony Frost was more fortunate. The eldest son of a Lancashire family, well established in the cotton industry, he was provided with ample means and had no necessity to work at all. The liberal allowance he received from his father enabled him to live in luxury with no more worries than those he had brought on himself through the publication of a thin volume of alleged poems that nobody understood, and which the critics treated as the biggest joke of the season.

In spite of these material, mental and physical differences, however, Jack and Tony got on very well together. It was their custom to spend Jack's annual holiday in some novel haunt usually well off the beaten track, and this summer they had come to the heart of the country where Tony, during one of his holiday-spot hunting expeditions, had hit upon Monk's Lodge, with a convenient 'To Let' board up.

For those who have a liking for rural solitude, the place was certainly ideal. Standing in its own old-world garden, and surrounded on three sides by heavily wooded hills, the cottage nestled snugly in the midst of typically wild Somerset scenery. The nearest village was two miles away, a little place called Friar's Vale that consisted of a public-house, two farms, and a handful of straggling cottages.

The site on which Monk's Lodge stood had, many years back, been occupied by a monastery. The ruined arch of the old building was still visible half-hidden among the trees, and close by was an irregular heap of the grey stone with which it had been built. On one side of the cottage was an extensive but much-neglected apple orchard; and beyond this, through a little gate, an overgrown and rather indistinct footpath wound its way through thick gorse till it reached the river Loam. It was more of a brook than a river, for at this point it was neither very deep nor very broad, its source originating locally in the small range of hills behind Monk's Lodge. Further down, however, it widened, and there was good fishing to be had, a peaceful sport of which Jack was especially fond, though Tony disliked it intensely. He preferred to lie at full length on the bank, and although he said on these occasions that he was engaged in composing sonnets, the strange noises that issued from his nostrils rather led Jack to doubt this statement.

They explored the cottage thoroughly, finding new delights at every turn; and then when they had exhausted the garden they decided to stroll down to the village with the object of obtaining some sort of domestic help. It was Jack who suggested dropping into the tumbledown post office-cum-general shop as a starting point.

'You'll be wanting to know someone as'll do for yer?' the old lady behind the counter asked when Jack had succeeded in impressing her with their requirements. 'An' where might ye be stayin'?'

5

'Monk's Lodge,' said Tony.

Immediately the old lady's manner changed. She started back as if her nose had accidentally touched a hot iron. 'Ye won't get nobody from 'ere as'll work at that place — no, not for no amount of money!' She lowered her voice to a dramatic whisper. 'It's evil, is Monk's Lodge, and 'aunted! No one round these parts'll go near it.'

'But — dash it all,' Tony protested. 'You don't really mean to tell me that you believe in that — that silly tosh!' he exclaimed.

'You can call it what yer like, sir,' said the old woman, shaking her head, 'but you won't get nobody 'ereabouts to go near Monk's Lodge, not if yer tries from now till doomsday!'

Jack exchanged an amused glance with Tony, and the latter was in the act of opening his mouth to say something further when a heavy footfall crossed the threshold of the little shop and a farm labourer lounged up to the counter.

'Give us an ounce of Nosegay, Mother,' he said, speaking in a broad Somersetshire dialect, and then noticing Tony and Jack he touched his shabby cap.

Jack nodded in return and gave the man a friendly smile, which prompted him to remark that it was nice weather and to inquire if they were staying in the village.

'We have just taken Monk's Lodge,' replied Jack, and he went on to explain that he was looking for someone who would keep the place clean and cook for them.

The villager's expression changed and, like the old lady, he shook his head. 'You won't get nobody to work for you up at the lodge,' he said decisively. 'Least not from Friar's Vale, you won't!'

'But there's nothing wrong with the place!' expostulated Tony irritably. 'This story about it being haunted is a lot of silly nonsense!'

The labourer leaned forward and prodded him in the chest with the butt end of a black clay pipe. 'Silly it may sound to you,' he replied solemnly, 'but you ain't lived in these parts, sir. There ain't man, woman nor child as 'ud go near that there place after nightfall, and there be precious few as 'ud go near it in the daytime!'

'But why?' demanded Tony, drawing back slightly so as to avoid being prodded again.

'What's the matter with it?'

'Things 'ave been 'appening,' said the labourer profoundly. 'Queer things! There's them what 'as seen things and 'eard things!'

'What things?' said Jack.

'Shadders flitting through the wood, lights that weren't made by no 'uman, and whisperings and suchlike. Why, it were only last night,' the villager continued, evidently warming to his subject, 'while I was 'aving me usual pint down at the Dovecote, that old Dinwood the postman came in all white and trembling and said as 'ow he'd seen the figure of a monk, robed and cowled, moving about up by the lodge.'

'Bosh!' said Tony rudely. 'Old Dinwood must have had one over the eight.'

''E don't drink at all as a rule, sir,' said the labourer, slowly filling his pipe from the tobacco he had just bought. 'But that ain't all. Perhaps you can say, sir, why the folks that bought Monk's Lodge only stayed there for six weeks?'

'I certainly can,' said Tony. 'The agent, Johnny, told me the whole business. The people who owned Monk's Lodge have gone to America for a holiday, and they are letting the place furnished while they're away.'

In spite of this plausible explanation, however, neither the villager nor the old lady appeared convinced. Notwithstanding all arguments to the contrary, they insisted that Jack and Tony were wasting their time trying to find anyone in Friar's Vale who would brave the mysterious unknown terrors of Monk's Lodge.

'Well,' said Jack after they had received the same reply from half a dozen different people in the village, 'there's only one thing for it. We shall have to get in some grub and look after ourselves.'

'I suppose that's the only solution,' remarked Tony dismally. 'But it's a dashed nuisance! I simply loathe fiddling about cooking. Let's get in as much tinned stuff as possible.'

As Jack privately thought he would loathe to eat any food that Tony had cooked, he did not argue this point. Over a pint of excellent beer at the local inn they made out a list of the things that they would require, and when this had been drastically cut down — for Tony was rather inclined to be lavish — they returned to the general shop

9

to make their purchases.

They arrived back at Monk's Lodge heavily laden and rather tired. Having had some tea and unpacked their various belongings, they spent the remainder of the day rambling about the garden, smoking and chatting.

Dusk merged into darkness, and presently, after an excellent supper, they went to bed without being disturbed by any of the horrific things which the gossip of the village might have led them to expect. In fact, it was not until the following night that the first of the series of strange happenings, which later were to end in tragedy, began.

It had been a scorching day, most of which had been spent in a voyage of exploration along the banks of the Loam, and darkness had already fallen when they got back to the cottage. They had something to eat, and then Jack sat down to write some letters while Tony wandered out into the garden to smoke.

It was a beautiful night; the moon high in the heavens draped the lawn and trees in a mantle of silver. That hushed stillness which only the country can provide lay over everything, unbroken except by the faint cheep-cheep of a bat as it circled overhead. Tony strolled to the end of the garden and paused by the ragged hedge that divided it from the wood. He had been there for perhaps three minutes, enjoying the beauty of the night, when suddenly a peculiar sensation stole over him. He felt that he was being watched. From somewhere in the darkness of the wood behind him he sensed invisible eyes looking at him. The feeling was so strong that he swung round, and then with a violent start he caught his breath, for through a gap in the hedge a white face was peering at him!

As he looked, it vanished, and he heard the sound of breaking twigs as footsteps padded swiftly through the wood. In three strides Tony was at the hedge, but the thickly growing trees made the darkness beyond intense and he could see nothing. It occurred to him to follow, but the wood was uninviting. After all, it was probably only some tramp who was prowling about in the hope of picking up a scrap of food. He made this suggestion to himself and tried to believe it. Yet there had been something so sinister about that white face watching from the darkness that the remembrance of it sent an unpleasant shiver down his spine, and he went back to the cottage at a much quicker pace than he had left it.

Jack had finished his second letter and was in the act of sealing it in an envelope when Tony came in. He listened with a smile while his friend related his experience.

'I'll bet you thought you had seen the ghost!' he chuckled.

'You wouldn't be so ready to laugh,' Tony remonstrated in rather injured voice, 'if you had been there. It was very unpleasant.'

'I expect it was only a tramp,' said Jack. 'Still, we'd better be careful and see that all the windows are fastened and the doors locked before we go to bed.'

And so the incident of the white face was dismissed, though later they were to remember it.

★　★　★

It was on the following morning that Tony received the letter. It was a rather odd communication, bearing the printed heading of a firm of estate agents in Dryseley, and which ran as follows:

Monk's Lodge,
Friar's Vale
Anthony Frost, Esq.
Dear Sir,
If it is convenient, I should like to call and have a chat with you at four o'clock tomorrow, Wednesday afternoon. There is something in connection with Monk's Lodge about which, I regret, I failed to enlighten you. The matter is very urgent, so I hope you will be able to see me.
Yours faithfully,
WILLIAM P. OGDEN.

'Dashed funny letter from Ogden,' Tony exclaimed, pushing it across the table to Jack. 'What do you make of it? Ogden is the agent I got this place from.'

Jack read the letter twice, then looked up with raised eyebrows. 'I don't know what it can be all about,' he said, 'unless there's some hitch in the agreement. Anyway, we'd better be in when he comes, so we'll have to modify our plans for the day.'

They had arranged to go on a fishing expedition, or rather, Jack had arranged to do the fishing while Tony looked on; but in the face of Mr. Ogden's letter they agreed that this should be postponed. There were several fresh things required for the larder — milk, butter, bread, etcetera — and after breakfast they went down into the village to get them.

About a mile outside Horton there was an empty cottage, and as they passed this they saw a Ford van drawn up outside. Two men were struggling up the narrow pathway with a heavy bookcase.

'Looks as if we're going to have neighbours,' remarked Jack casually.

'By Jove, you're right,' said Tony, gazing hard at a spot beyond the van. 'And very nice, too!'

Jack followed the direction of his friend's glance and saw the cause of the last remark. Standing on the far side of the van was an elderly man. He was tall and wore a panama hat and the loose black neck-tie that is usually associated with Chelsea. Beside him — and the reason for Tony's sudden attention — stood a woman.

She was quite young — Jack guessed her age at twenty-one — and more than ordinarily pretty.

She looked round as they passed, and for a brief instant her eyes met Jack's. It may have been his imagination, but he thought that they held a mute questioning — almost an appealing — look. It was only for an instant, then she turned away.

They waited at the lodge the whole of that afternoon for Mr. Ogden, but he never came. Either the urgent matter he had mentioned had proved not to be so important after all, or some other and more pressing business had detained him. Whatever the cause, Jack, not unreasonably, felt annoyed. The day's outing had been ruined, and he spent the evening in a particularly bad temper, eventually going off to bed early and leaving Tony struggling valiantly with a new poem, the inspiration for which had been provided by the woman they had seen that morning.

Now, Tony could not write poetry, and nobody had any illusions on that point except Tony himself. And by two o'clock in the morning, when he had filled the waste-paper basket with spoilt sheets and the lamp was burning low for want of oil, Tony began to believe that he could not either. With an exclamation of disgust he rose and stretched himself, and was in the act of blowing out the light, preparatory to going to bed, when from outside the window came a soft crunching sound, like the sound of stealthy footsteps on gravel.

He listened tensely, but the noise was not repeated, and going over to the window he pulled aside the curtains, letting in a flood of moonlight. And then he stepped back quickly, with a startled exclamation, for written in crimson across the upper half of the windowpane were the words:

'THERE IS DANGER. GO WHILE YOU CAN!'

And they looked as though they had been written by a finger dipped in blood.

2

Mr. Trevor Lowe

Monk's Lodge,
Near Friar's Vale,
Somerset.
7th August.
My Dear Lowe,

I don't for a moment expect that you will be able to accept this invitation, knowing how busy you usually are; but if you *have* got any spare time hanging on your hands, I should be awfully pleased if you could come down and stay here for a while. To be quite frank, the most extraordinary things have been happening here during the past few days; and, knowing your tremendous interest in anything abnormal or outside the general run of life, I'm certain you would enjoy yourself. I won't tell you anything more until I see you — if I do see you!

I am staying here with Jack Denton, whom you may have heard me mention but whom I don't think you have ever met. We are quite alone, but I think we can make you tolerably comfortable. Monk's Lodge is a very old place — part of a ruined monastery, and apart from anything else — and there is a great deal more — I know that will interest you immensely. Come at once if you can, and if you want to work bring your secretary with you. If you let us know what train you are coming by, we will meet you at King's Hayling station.

Do come.

Yours sincerely,

TONY FROST.

That famous dramatist, Mr. Trevor Lowe, read the letter over his breakfast and then handed it across the table to his friend and secretary, Arnold White. 'What do you make of that?' he asked with his characteristic one-sided smile.

White glanced quickly through the contents and noted the signature. 'Tony Frost? Isn't he the eldest son of the Lancashire cotton mill owner?' he asked.

'That's the fellow,' said Lowe, nodding and reaching for the toast and marmalade. 'His father financed that last play of mine. His son's a charming chap. Looks a fool, but isn't.'

White read the letter again. 'Wonder what he means by extraordinary happenings?' he queried.

The dramatist helped himself to some marmalade. 'I have no more idea than the man in the moon,' he declared. 'But it certainly sounds interesting.'

'Apart from the interest side,' said White, 'the holiday would do you good.'

'I was thinking the same thing myself,' replied Lowe, munching his toast. 'We've finished the play — there's only that film to complete —'

'And there's a month yet before that's due,' said his secretary. 'So there's no need to worry about it for the moment. You've been working at pretty high pressure, and you need a change of some sort.'

'With the possibility of a little excitement thrown in,' said Lowe with a smile, after which he finished his toast and searched in the pocket of his dressing-gown for his pipe.

'Well, I haven't had any of *that* kind of excitement since that business with Shadgold. By Jove, I wonder if these 'extraordinary happenings' are likely to lead to anything half as exciting?' He rose and, going over to a side table, began to fill his pipe from a big jade-green tobacco jar.

Arnold White looked across at the back of his employer and smiled to himself. He remembered the 'business with Shadgold' not altogether with unadulterated pleasure, for it had been a hectic and dangerous time for both of them.

Trevor Lowe had decided to write a crime play, and in order to secure the necessary detail had consulted his friend Inspector Shadgold of Scotland Yard. Shadgold was at the time investigating the murder of Thomas Carraway, the ex-member of Parliament who had been found stabbed to death in the grounds of his house in the country. He suggested that Lowe would acquire all knowledge he wanted if he accompanied him on the case. Trevor Lowe had eagerly agreed, and the result had been that when Shadgold had found himself completely at sea, the dramatist, with his keen sense for detail, had solved the mystery. It brought him no little publicity, for the crime was a sensational one. His photograph appeared in all the newspapers in the unaccustomed position of being chief witness in a notorious murder case, and the gross takings of one of his plays that was running at the time doubled themselves. Ever since that time he had taken a tremendous interest in any case that Shadgold was concerned with, and the inspector had a habit of dropping in and discussing any particular problem which was worrying him.

'I should think it unlikely that this would turn out to be anything like the Carraway affair,' remarked White as Lowe struck a match and lit his pipe.

'I should think so, too,' replied the dramatist. 'But still, you never know. Anyway, I shall go, and hope for the best. You might see how the trains run.'

White went over to the desk and consulted a Bradshaw. Presently he looked up from the book. 'There's a fast train at eleven fifteen,' he said. 'That ought to enable us to arrive at Monk's Lodge in time for tea.'

'Me to arrive,' corrected Lowe quietly. 'You're not coming!'

White looked surprised. 'Why?' he asked.

'Because,' answered the dramatist, 'when you do come, I would like you to bring the car with you, and they haven't finished repairing that cracked cylinder head yet.'

'I see,' said White. 'Shall I wire Frost that you're coming down?'

His employer nodded. 'Yes, do,' he said.

Trevor Lowe arrived at Paddington shortly after eleven, and having secured a first-class ticket through to King's Hayling, stopped at the bookstall to buy one or two papers. The train was not crowded, and he had no difficulty in finding a corner seat in a first-class compartment adjoining the luncheon car. He handed the obliging porter, who had looked after his suitcase, a tip that brought a smile to that official's not very prepossessing face, and settled down for the journey.

Punctually at eleven fifteen, the guard blew his whistle; and with a deluge of steam, and a wailing of brakes, the Western Express got under way. And while Lowe read his papers and the train thundered along the steel track to its destination, a telegraph boy set out from King's Hayling on a bicycle. He carried in his pouch a telegram addressed to Tony Frost, stating the time of Lowe's arrival, and signed by White; and in spite of the urgency with which all wires are supposed to be treated, the boy did not overexert himself. He pedalled at a leisurely pace along the dusty country roads, tunelessly whistling snatches from the latest fox-trot that the radio was popularising at the time. Reaching Friar's Vale eventually, he stopped to ask the way to Monk's Lodge, and the look of disgust that crossed his face when he was told that it was two miles further on was a study fit for a cartoonist! He was no longer whistling when he remounted his bicycle.

It was no joke riding the six miles to Friar's Vale and back again on a scorching day like this. His collar was already limp and clammy, and the sight of a steep and rough incline before him did nothing to restore his good humour.

'Fancy living in a blinking 'ole like this,' he muttered as he began to negotiate the hill. 'People who live orf the earth 'aven't no right to 'ave telegrams!'

As the incline grew steeper, he began to tack from side to side of the road, hoping by this means to lighten his progress. Unfortunately, during one of these erratic manoeuvres the front wheel of the bicycle came in contact with a sharp flint, and with a hissing sigh the tyre went flat.

'That's torn it,' grunted the boy, with no intention of being funny; and getting off his machine, he stood staring at it while he wiped his streaming face with a grubby handkerchief.

He was still contemplating the useless bicycle when a man came round the bend in the road, walking briskly. He was broad-shouldered and thick-set, and his rather pale complexion was accentuated by the little black pointed beard that concealed his chin.

'What's the matter, my lad? Had an accident?' He spoke smoothly and slowly, but his dark eyes were eager and alert, and they took in every detail of the boy's official uniform.

The telegraph boy explained what had happened.

'You were going to Monk's Lodge, were you?' said the newcomer thoughtfully, and then he smiled. 'I'm going past there myself, so if you like I'll take the telegram for you while you set to work and mend your puncture.'

The boy hesitated. It was against regulations, but it would save a lot of trouble; and, after all, it was doubtful anybody would find out.

'You're a sport, you are, guv'nor,' he said suddenly, making up his mind. He fumbled in the leather pouch at his side and, taking out the buff envelope, handed it to the man with the beard. 'It's for a Mr. Frost,' he said unnecessarily.

'All right, I'll deliver it,' said the man, slipping it into his pocket; and, leaving the boy to wrestle with the damaged tyre, he went on up the hill.

The moment he got out of sight of the boy, however, his calm manner deserted him. With eager but careful fingers he unsealed the flap of the envelope, taking the utmost pains not to tear it, and withdrew the contents.

When he had finished reading the brief

message, he put the telegram back and carefully resealed the envelope. And as he went on to Monk's Lodge, his dark brows were drawn together in an angry frown, and his thin lips were compressed so tightly that they had the appearance of a scarlet scratch above the blackness of his beard.

★　★　★

Tony Frost found the telegram lying on the front doormat when he and Jack returned to the cottage for lunch after a morning's fishing, and there was nothing in its appearance to show that it had been tampered with.

'I bet this is from Lowe!' he exclaimed, picking it up and ripping it open. 'Yes, it is, by Jove!' he went on after he had glanced at it. 'He's coming on the Western Express, and arrives at King's Hayling this afternoon.'

'We'd better have lunch right away, then,' said Jack, 'otherwise we shan't get there in time for the train, and we don't want to keep Lowe hanging about.'

They had a hasty lunch of tinned

tongue and tomatoes, and arrived at King's Hayling, hot and dusty, after their six-mile tramp, ten minutes before the train was due in.

'We can't expect Lowe to walk back,' said Tony. 'He'll have luggage and things. We'd better see if we can't get hold of a car of some sort.'

'There you are — that's what you want,' said Jack. 'That car looks as if it might be for hire.'

Drawn up at the kerb outside the station entrance was a rather dilapidated car. It was the only vehicle standing there, for cabs were an unknown luxury in King's Hayling, and a gloomy-looking individual who was sitting on the running-board, studying the racing columns of the *Somersetshire Sun*, looked up as they approached.

'Want a car, sir?' he asked quickly.

'Yes.' Tony explained that he was expecting a friend by the London train and wanted a conveyance to take them back to Monk's Lodge.

'Never 'eard of it!' said the driver, scratching his head. 'But if it's near Friar's Vale, I'll do the run for 'alf a quid.'

They clinched the deal at once, and turned into the station. There were still seven minutes to wait, and to pass the time Jack bought a copy of the local paper. He was glancing casually down the front page when an item in the bottom right-hand corner attracted his attention. Under the heading, 'Strange Disappearance of a Dryseley Man', the paragraph ran:

★　★　★

'The strange disappearance of a Dryseley estate agent is causing a good deal of interest and not a little alarm. The missing man is a Mr. William P. Ogden, aged forty-seven, a bachelor living in North Rise, Dryseley. A clerk in the employ of the firm, of which Mr. Ogden is the head, stated that after lunch on Wednesday last Mr. Ogden left the office on some mission, the details of which he did not disclose. Since then nothing has been seen or heard of Mr. Ogden. It is feared that he may be wandering somewhere suffering from loss of memory ...'

★　★　★

There followed a photograph and a description of Mr. Ogden, with a request that anyone able to supply information should do so to the Dryseley police superintendent.

Jack caught Tony by the arm and pushed the newspaper in front of him. 'Read that!' he directed, stabbing with his finger at the paragraph, and there was a queer harshness about his voice. 'That accounts for his failing to keep his appointment the other afternoon!'

Tony's expression changed as he read the brief news item. 'This is dashed queer,' he commented seriously. 'I'm blessed if I know what to make of it all.'

The shrill scream of a train-whistle stopped Jack from making any reply. A feather of smoke in the distance heralded the approach of the Western Express, and a few seconds later the train came, clanking and hissing, into the station.

Jack and Tony started down the platform as it drew to a standstill, eagerly watching the people getting out. Almost the first passenger to alight was Trevor Lowe, and as he caught sight of Tony he smiled and waved. The latter dashed up and gripped his hand.

'I say, Lowe,' he exclaimed breathlessly, 'I'm glad to see you. Awfully decent of you to come. Only a cottage, you know — have to take pot luck and all that!' He checked his torrent for a moment and grabbed Jack by the arm. 'Meet my friend, Jack Denton,' he went on. 'Jack, this is Trevor Lowe.'

The dramatist shook hands and exchanged a few words with Jack while Tony signalled a porter.

'We've got a car outside,' said Tony as he succeeded in attracting the porter's attention; the man came up and took charge of Lowe's luggage. 'Come on!' He led the way out of the station and, after instructing the porter to put the bag in the front of the car with the driver, the three of them got into the back.

The car was not much to look at, but it went quite well, and was soon running towards Friar's Vale at a steady twenty miles an hour. The afternoon was perfect; and to Lowe, who had not been out of London for over six months, the air and beauty of the countryside was very pleasant. He allowed himself to relax against the upholstery and turned to Tony.

'Well,' he said, with a smile, 'what about these 'queer happenings' you mentioned in your letter? Let's hear about them — or was that just put in as an inducement to get me to come down?'

'It certainly was not,' replied Tony indignantly, and with the help of Jack he proceeded to give Lowe an outline of the events that had taken place, concluding by showing him the news paragraph in the local paper.

The dramatist read the item carefully, read it through a second time, and then laid the paper on his knee in silence. Jack, who had expected him to make some kind of comment, was rather surprised when he did nothing of the sort. In fact, his next remark seemed to be totally irrelevant to the thing they had been discussing.

'How far is Monk's Lodge from Friar's Vale?' he asked after what seemed a lengthy pause.

'A little over two miles,' answered Jack, and Tony nodded in confirmation.

Lowe asked no further questions, but

appeared lost in a contemplation of the surrounding scenery. The road, at this point of their journey, wound and twisted between high banks that rose on either side to thickly wooded hills. Before them was a sharp bend, and beyond that the road sloped steeply upwards. The driver, who was evidently familiar with the way, sounded his horn, took the corner carefully, and then pressed his foot hard on the accelerator in order to take the hill ahead. The car engine roared noisily, and the machine bounded forward with a jolting motion that almost threw Lowe and his companions off the seat. The ancient springs squeaked and groaned painfully as the wheels bumped over the rough surface.

'By Jove!' gasped Tony. 'I'm bruised all over!'

Lowe said nothing. He had twisted round and was peering with a rather stern face at the back padding of the seat. Jack turned also to see what he was looking at, and as he did so the dramatist leaned a little sideways and plunged the thumb and forefinger of his right hand into a small tear in the leather upholstery, close to where his head had been.

'What are you looking for?' asked Jack.

'This!' answered Lowe shortly, and held out his hand. In the centre of his open palm was a bullet, jagged and flattened by the vicious force of its impact.

'How did that get there — what's it for?' asked Tony in surprise.

Trevor Lowe's lips curled slowly in a rather hard smile. 'What's it for —?' he repeated softly. 'I rather think somebody meant it for me!'

3

The Locked Room

Trevor Lowe leaned back in his chair and smoked thoughtfully. He was seated by the open window that overlooked the garden of Monks Lodge. Outside, the late-afternoon sun was already casting long grotesque shadows on the lawn, and touching the distant vista of the woods with the mellow gold of approaching evening. Lowe, however, saw nothing of the beauty of the scene before him. With his level brows contracted to a deep frown, he was thinking busily.

He was a man of middle height, dark, with greying hair at the temples and clean-shaven. His face, without in any way being handsome, was very pleasant; and when he smiled — as he did very readily — his smile was truly delightful. In spite of his success, he had never acquired that air of conscious superiority that marks — and mars — so many men of his profession; but at the same time no one who came in contact with him could fail to realise that this was no ordinary man. He seemed in some indefinable way to exude a tremendous sense of latent power. His chief asset might be described in one word: charm — a rare and subtle thing, but a thing which Trevor Lowe possessed in abundance.

When he had accepted Tony Frost's invitation, it had been more with a view to enjoying the quiet relaxation offered by a few days in the country than to any interest in the queer happenings that Tony had hinted at in his letter, and which at the time he had believed to be merely some trifling affair, if not existing wholly in Tony's fertile imagination. And yet within half an hour of his arrival in Somerset, an attempt had been made on his life by someone wielding a rifle!

It required no very great intelligence to guess how the would-be assassin had planned the attack. He had been hiding somewhere among the trees when the car bearing the party to Monk's Lodge had rounded the sharp bend just before taking the hill that led to Friar's Vale. It was an ideal spot for the purpose. The car had of necessity to slow down considerably at the corner, enabling the shooter to take careful aim. The rifle, of course, had been fitted with a silencer, and the slight 'plop' it must have made had been drowned by the noise of the engine. But he had felt the wind of the bullet as it whistled by his head, and the smack as it struck the back of the seat.

To say that Lowe was in the least degree scared would be an exaggeration, but he was not foolhardy, and in that shot he had read a warning not to be ignored. Why his life should be attempted at all, in the circumstances, was a mystery; but that it was connected in some way with the happenings related by Tony he did not doubt for a moment.

Two things stood out clearly: the unknown shooter must have had knowledge of his arrival, and there was something very extraordinary going on around Monk's Lodge.

Tapping the ashes of his pipe on the window-sill, Lowe rose leisurely and stood for a moment looking about the room. It was a comfortable place, made mellow by time. In the centre there was a long, polished oak refectory table and half a dozen ancient carved chairs. The ceiling was low, and supported by heavy beams, which had the effect of making the room appear longer than it was. The only carpeting was a small rectangular rug in front of the wide fireplace, the rest of the floor being of plain polished natural oak. The walls were a distempered russet colour above the oak panelling, and at the far end of the room was a sideboard, its slightly warped shelves littered with specimens of old pewter.

It was at his own wish that he had remained alone this afternoon — the one following his arrival. The others had tried hard to persuade him to go fishing with them, but he had refused. He wanted to have a good look round at Monk's Lodge and he wanted to explore the place by himself. The warning on the window could only have been put there with one object: for some reason or other, somebody wanted to get Jack and Tony out of the cottage. Unless the whole thing was a practical joke — and the attempt on his life precluded this possibility — there was no other reasonable explanation. Therefore, it seemed more than probable that within the precincts of Monk's Lodge would be found the clue to the whole business.

For twenty minutes or so Lowe explored the ground floor, digging into every nook and cranny; and when he had exhausted this part of the cottage he mounted the stairs and turned his attention to the upper part. He had made a thorough search of the room occupied by Tony and Jack, and was walking along the short corridor that led to his own room when he paused at a small window that looked out onto the garden. From this window it was possible to see odd patches of the winding path that led up to the cottage from the direction of Friar's Vale, and it was something moving along this path that had caught his eye and caused him to pause at the window.

Watching, he saw through a gap in the hedge the vivid splash of colour that had attracted his attention. It was a woman in a yellow beret and a canary-coloured pullover. She was walking slowly, glancing to left and right, and he watched her movements curiously.

At the gate that led into the garden she paused, apparently to admire the house; but after a moment's hesitation, and again glancing quickly about, she opened the gate and slipped through. As though her sole object was interest in the garden, she strolled in a leisurely fashion up the path, and presently veered slightly until her direction brought her close by the window of the room where Lowe had previously sat.

Almost opposite this window was a large flowerbed. Here she stopped and, to Lowe's surprise, began searching rapidly among the tangled mass of flowers. After a second or two she straightened up, slipping something into the pocket of her jumper. Lowe could not see what it was, but he was determined if possible to find out, and leaving the window he went hurriedly down the stairs.

But by the time he reached the garden, the woman had gone; nor was there any sign of her on the white ribbon of road. Somewhere near at hand, however, he heard the whine of a car, and guessed that it was by this means that she had been able to get out of sight so quickly.

He went back into the cottage to continue his exploration rather thoughtfully. Another peculiar incident had been added to the list that was so rapidly mounting up, though at that moment the dramatist had no premonition of the tragic conclusion to which they were leading.

He examined all the rooms carefully without the slightest result, and then came to a door that was locked. It was in all probability a lumber-room containing odds and ends of no interest to anybody except the owners of the cottage. But still Lowe was curious to see what it contained. He tried the keys of the other doors, but none of them would fit. The lock was apparently a patent one, and he concluded it had most likely been put on by the owners of the cottage in order to safeguard their personal property from the prying eyes of possible tenants while they were away.

He was making his way downstairs again when Jack and Tony returned. Although they looked tired, they appeared to have had a good day, for the basket Jack was carrying was bulging with fish.

'By the way, Lowe,' said Tony, suddenly

breaking in on a remark of Jack's when they were having tea a few minutes later, 'we rang up the police station at Dryseley and told them about Ogden's failure to keep his appointment.'

'What did they say?' asked Lowe. 'Have they found him yet?'

'No,' said Tony. 'There's not a sign of the fellow anywhere.'

'It's certainly curious,' muttered the dramatist, absently stirring his tea.

'It's more than curious,' said Jack. 'This man Ogden must be somewhere. He can't have vanished into thin air.'

'That, apparently, is exactly what he has done,' said Lowe. 'Of course, there are several possible explanations. We know nothing of Ogden's private life whatsoever. He may have a very good reason for wanting to disappear.'

'Then you think he went of his own free will?' said Jack.

'I didn't say so,' replied Lowe. 'I was merely pointing out that it was possible. By the way,' he went on, 'do either of you happen to know a rather pretty woman staying around here?'

Tony looked across at Jack and winked. 'We certainly know of one,' he replied carefully, 'don't we, Jack?'

His friend flushed slightly beneath his tan. 'Er — yes — I — er — certainly,' he said, and looked across at Lowe inquiringly. 'Why?'

The dramatist was filling his pipe carefully. 'She called here today while you were out,' he remarked. 'I was wondering if either of you knew who she was.'

'Called here?' gasped Tony in surprise. 'What did she want?'

'I don't know,' said Lowe, 'but whatever it was, she apparently found it.'

They listened interestedly while he told them what he had seen from the upstairs window.

'What was the woman like?' asked Tony when Lowe had finished.

'She was fair, of medium height, rather slim, and decidedly attractive,' answered Lowe.

'It must be the same woman that we saw outside Dinwood's cottage,' said Jack, turning to Tony.

'Certainly sounds like it,' agreed his

friend. 'I haven't seen any other woman round here who would answer to that description.'

'Who is she?' asked Lowe.

Jack explained where they had first seen the woman. 'I can't think what she's doing here, or what she was looking for,' he went on in a puzzled tone.

'Neither can I,' said the dramatist. 'I'm rather under the impression that she thought everyone was out. However, it makes another little unexplained incident to add to our list.'

'I wish we could get to the bottom of it all,' remarked Tony. 'I hate living in the atmosphere of a shilling shocker.'

'I'm afraid you will have to be patient,' said Lowe with a smile. 'We can do nothing at present except wait. At the moment we are rather in the position of a person who has been given a jigsaw puzzle with half the pieces missing. We haven't got enough data to form any theory or to make any concrete move. I'm convinced that all these peculiar incidents are leading to something definite, and that there will be a fresh development sooner or later that will supply us with something to get a grip on. In the mean-time, all we can do is to wait and watch.'

'It's all darned queer,' complained Jack. 'That shot on the way from the station, for instance. Who on earth was responsible for that, and why should they want to try to murder you?'

'I haven't the least idea,' Lowe said, 'unless somebody has recognised me in connection with the Carraway affair and thinks I'm up to my old games again. It certainly points to one thing, however — something big is either happening or going to happen here, and my presence is considered a danger by the people who are planning it. I should —'

He stopped suddenly and glanced swiftly across at Jack and Tony. A heavy thud had sounded directly overhead — so heavy that flaky particles of the ceiling floated down between them onto the table. Lowe was on his feet immediately, and the others were not slow to follow his example.

'What the dickens was that?' queried Tony, and his face in the twilight of the room was visibly paler.

'Light the lamp,' said Lowe sharply,

and his hand fumbled in his pocket for his lighter. 'What room is just overhead?'

'The lumber-room,' answered Jack. 'Here, Tony — I've got some matches!'

Tony took the box he held out and lit the lamp, for the dusk had crept on while they had been sitting talking.

'The locked room!' whispered Lowe under his breath. He crossed to the door. 'Come on — and bring the light! We'll see if we can find out what that noise was.'

At the top of the stairs Tony held the lamp so that Lowe could see, and the dramatist tried the handle of the lumber-room door. It was still locked.

'I'm going to bust the door open,' he said, and launched his whole weight against the panel. But the door held. Like the rest of the woodwork in Monk's Lodge, it was made of seasoned oak, and it took the combined efforts of Lowe and Jack before, with a splintering, rending sound, it crashed open.

Trevor Lowe was the first to cross the threshold of the room beyond, and he narrowly missed tripping over something that lay on the floor. 'Tony — the light, quick!' he shouted.

Tony came in, the flare of the lamp in his hand jumping fitfully in the draught. The small room was littered with old boxes, but it was what occupied the centre of the floor that riveted the attention of the dramatist. Beside an overturned chair lay the huddled figure of a man, face downwards!

With a little sharp intake of his breath, Lowe bent down and laid his hand on the motionless form. It was stiff and rigid, and the hand he touched was icy cold. He turned the body gently over until the light from the lamp fell full upon the dead face, and then Tony gave a hoarse cry.

'Good God!' he exclaimed huskily. 'It's Mr. Ogden!'

Lowe looked at the bloodstains on the chair and on the floor around it. They had long since congealed, proving that Mr. William P. Ogden had been dead for some time!

4

The Woman Who Screamed

Inspector Jesson of the local police sucked the point of his pencil and flipped the pages of his notebook with a large and not particularly clean thumb. 'This is a serious business, gentlemen,' he announced, shaking his head with ponderous gravity. 'A very serious business!'

'We are aware of that,' replied Lowe. 'Murder usually is a serious business.'

The inspector looked at him doubtfully, as if not quite certain how to treat the remark.

The hour was late, well past midnight, and Lowe, the local inspector, Tony and Jack were gathered in the dining-room of Monk's Lodge. Upstairs, Dr. MacGuire, the divisional surgeon, was engaged in examining all that remained of the unfortunate estate agent, while a shuffling of feet in the hall testified to the impatience of the police constable who stood on guard at the front door.

The sudden and startling discovery of the dead man in the locked lumber-room had provided an unexpected climax to the series of what Tony had called 'queer happenings'. The dead man had obviously been locked in the room for several days. Lowe was able to tell that from the state of the body, and the blood stains, without waiting for confirmation of the medical evidence. Death had been caused by a heavy blow to the back of the head. The base of the skull was crushed to pulp, and it was probable that death had come so swiftly that Mr. Ogden had never seen the hand that struck him down.

The discovery of the body might have been postponed almost indefinitely, but for the fact that something had upset its balance and caused it to topple out of the chair on which it had been propped.

A cursory examination of the room had revealed nothing in the nature of a clue to the murderer's identity — although, so far as the motive was concerned, it did not require a great deal of intelligence to connect this with the appointment that the estate agent had never kept. Mr. Ogden had become possessed, or was about to reveal, some knowledge already in his possession, that was dangerous to the person behind this strange business. That was the fairly obvious conclusion to be drawn from the letter he had written to Tony Frost. As to what this knowledge had been, Lowe was completely in the dark. Nor, at this early stage, did he feel inclined to hazard a guess. Inspector Shadgold had read him many lectures about theorising without facts. It was easy to unconsciously twist the facts to suit the theories, instead of making the theories suit the facts.

Standing in the room of death while Tony had gone off to inform the police, Lowe hurriedly ran through the actual facts that were in his possession, and found that they were unpleasantly meagre. There was the man whom Tony had seen peering through the hedge, and who might quite possibly have been only a tramp and nothing to do with the affair at all. There was the letter written by Mr. Ogden that, in light of the discovery of that night, was quite definitely connected with the problem. Then there was the scrawled warning on the window, the shot that had only missed Lowe by a fraction of an inch, and the strange behaviour of the woman in the garden, and finally the discovery of the dead man in the locked room.

There was some thread, invisible at the moment, that linked all these incidents together, and Lowe was still occupied in trying to discover a starting point from which to begin his investigation, when Tony's arrival with the police forced him to shelve the subject for the time being.

'Yes, it's a very serious matter,' remarked Inspector Jesson for the third time, 'and I should like you to answer a few questions. Which of you was the first to discover the crime?'

'I was actually the first to enter the room,' answered Lowe.

Inspector Jesson nodded. 'Right then, sir; I'll begin with you,' he said. 'What's your name?'

'Trevor Lowe,' answered the dramatist.

The bull-like head of the inspector jerked up. 'Eh? You don't happen, by any chance, to be *the* Mr. Trevor Lowe, do you?'

'I'm not aware,' replied the dramatist, 'of anyone else possessing the name.'

'I've heard about you,' said the inspector, writing laboriously in his notebook. 'You're a playwright, aren't you?'

'I've had some experience in that profession,' answered Lowe with a smile. The inspector was obviously preparing to fire off a battery of questions, and nobody knew better than he what little result would be gained by this tedious routine work. It was a sheer waste of time, though he realised that the official was merely complying with the regulations, and therefore he did his best to conceal his impatience.

'Are you staying in the house?' asked the inspector.

'Yes; I'm a guest of Mr. Frost and Mr. Denton,' replied Lowe, and he proceeded to relate what had brought him to Monk's Lodge. He did not mention the shot from the hillside, a fact which Jack and Tony noticed.

The inspector listened attentively, and raised his rather bushy eyebrows when he heard about the warning on the window. 'You ought to 'ave reported that to the police,' he muttered, glaring across at Tony. ''Owever, it can't be 'elped now. Did you know the dead man?' he went on, addressing Lowe.

'I have never seen him before in my life,' Lowe answered.

'How do you suppose he came to be in that room?' asked the inspector after he had noted down Lowe's previous reply.

'My suppositions are not evidence, you know,' pointed out Lowe gently. 'But I suggest he was put there by the person who killed him.'

The inspector's rather florid face went the colour of a newly boiled beetroot. 'Um — yes — very likely!' he growled. 'Now, I understand he had an appointment to see Mr. Frost on the afternoon of Wednesday last?'

'Yes, that's right,' put in Tony, 'and he never kept it.'

The inspector turned and looked at him with great dignity. 'I'll deal with you presently,' he said. 'One witness at a time, if you please.'

He repeated his question to Lowe, and the dramatist replied in the affirmative.

'That is so far as I know,' he added a trifle maliciously. 'I had not arrived then.'

'Oh!' Inspector Jesson appeared a trifle nonplussed. 'Then you don't know whether he kept his appointment or not?'

'Dash it all!' interrupted Tony, 'I've just told you he didn't!'

The inspector drew himself up to his full height. 'If I 'ave any more interruptions from you, sir,' he said, frowning, 'I shall 'ave to ask you to leave the room!'

'But —' Tony was beginning, when a sign from Lowe stopped him, and he subsided.

Inspector Jesson cleared his throat. 'Now,' he said, glancing at his notebook, 'about this appointment. Mr. Ogden left his office after lunch on Wednesday with the intention of coming 'ere to Monk's Lodge, and these gentlemen —' He indicated Jack and Tony with a wave of his fat hand. '—say 'e never arrived. Now what proof have we of that?'

'The fact that they say so is sufficient proof for me,' said Lowe.

'But it isn't for me, sir,' declared the inspector. 'I'm investigating an 'orrible crime, and it looks to me very suspicious — very suspicious indeed.' He paused and wagged his head from side to side, reminding Lowe of a performing seal that he had once seen in a circus.

'Here is a man,' the inspector went on, 'who sets out from his office to keep an appointment. From that moment he disappears, and several days after 'e's found murdered in a locked room in the very 'ouse where he was going to when 'e left his office. The occupants of the 'ouse state that he never arrived. As I said before, it's very suspicious.'

'Are you accusing us of having murdered the fellow?' demanded Jack hotly.

'No, sir,' said the inspector. 'At the moment I'm not accusing anybody. I'm merely stating facts, and there's no getting away from those! Mr. Ogden left 'is office to come 'ere, and when 'is dead body was found it was found in this 'ouse.'

'You have overlooked the fact, Inspector,' said Lowe, 'that there's a considerable distance between Dryseley and Monk's Lodge. The fact that Mr. Ogden left his office with the intention of coming here is not proof that he ever arrived here — alive.'

'What do you mean?' asked the inspector.

'I mean,' replied the dramatist, 'that I'm practically convinced that the dead man was not killed inside the house at all.'

The inspector's jaw dropped, and he stared at Lowe with dumb surprise. ''Ave you any reason for saying that, sir?'

'Yes; a reason that you can verify for yourself, if you take another look at the body,' said Lowe. 'If you examine the back of Ogden's coat, you'll find several short blades of grass and traces of mud that have become stuck to the cloth with dried blood.'

The inspector licked his lips. 'Then it's your idea that the crime was committed outside?' he said.

'I'm certain of it,' Lowe answered.

'Um!' The inspector scratched one of his many chins. It was easy to see what was passing through his brain. He had come to the conclusion that Tony and Jack were responsible for the death of Ogden, and he was by no means pleased to have any obstacles put in the way of this theory. After all, this was probably the first time he had been associated with a murder case. His official duties, as a rule, were concerned with such petty crimes as fruit-stealing and the robbery of chicken runs. It would be a distinct feather in his cap if he could bring the case to a successful conclusion by arresting the criminals within a few hours of being called in to investigate the crime.

Suddenly his expression brightened. After all, the mere fact that the murder might have been committed outside instead of inside Monk's Hollow did not make so very much difference. It did not matter whether Ogden had been killed in the garden or whether he had been killed in the dining-room; those two town chaps were implicated just the same.

He was just about to put these thoughts into words when the door opened and the divisional surgeon entered. He was a wiry little man — Lowe put his age between fifty-five and sixty — with gold-rimmed spectacles and a quick, bird-like, rather furtive manner. The dramatist wondered whether he was very popular with his patients, for he was not at all the type one would expect to find as a general practitioner in a village like Friar's Vale. Country people are usually more likely to respond to a medical practitioner of the bland and jovial variety. He learned later that Dr. MacGuire had only been in Friar's Vale for the past six months, and so far from being popular he was most heartily disliked by the inhabitants, so much so that his practice was microscopic.

'I've finished,' he snapped, addressing the inspector, and his manner was abrupt, almost to the point of rudeness. 'Death was caused by a heavy blow on the head with some blunt instrument. Considerable force must have been used, for the back of the skull is smashed like an eggshell. That is all I can tell you until after the post-mortem.'

'Have you any idea how long he's been dead?' inquired Lowe.

The divisional surgeon turned a pair of small, piercing eyes on the dramatist and stared at him as if trying to decide whether he would answer or not.

'This is Mr. Trevor Lowe, Doctor,' interjected Inspector Jesson, with a jerk of his head. 'The writer. I expect you've 'eard of 'im.'

'Yes, of course, certainly,' snapped the little man, but without showing much interest. 'How long has the man been dead, you asked. It's impossible to tell at the moment. There'll have to be an autopsy. I can't say with any degree of certainty.'

'But approximately?' persisted Lowe.

'Maybe two, maybe three, maybe four days,' snapped the doctor irritably. 'Certainly not less than two.' He turned his back rudely on the dramatist, and addressed his next remark to Inspector Jesson. 'You won't want me anymore, will you? I'll let you have a preliminary report in the morning.'

All right, Doctor,' said the inspector.

With a jerk of his head, the little man crammed on his hat and took his departure.

Inspector Jesson's rather prominent eyes strayed to the closing door. 'Peculiar chap,' he muttered as he made a note in his book. 'Never know how to take him.' He closed the notebook with a snap and rubbed his upper lip with the end of his pencil. 'I don't think I can do much more here,' he said, 'so I think I'll be getting back to the station. Of course, I shall have to leave the constable on duty, and I must also request that none of you gentlemen leave until after the inquest.' He looked at each of them in turn.

'That's understood, Inspector,' said Lowe. 'You have my assurance that we shall be here when you want us.'

The others did not reply. Tony Frost's face wore an expression of harassed perplexity, and Jack, too, looked rather uncomfortable, though he did not show it quite so much as his friend. They both realised the cloud under which the murder of Ogden had put them, and both felt the unpleasantness of the situation.

'I shall have to go over and see the chief constable at King's Hayling,' continued the inspector as he prepared to take his leave. 'It looks to me as if we should have to get the assistance of the Yard on this job. It's a bit bigger than any I've handled before.'

'I think it is,' said Lowe; 'and unless I'm very much mistaken it's likely to prove considerably bigger than you imagine.'

The inspector looked at him, and his eyes opened wide. 'Do you by any chance know anything you haven't told me about?' he demanded.

The dramatist shook his head. 'No,' he replied. 'I'm merely expressing my own personal opinion. This crime —' He stopped suddenly, leaning forward in a listening attitude, and then they heard the sound which had interrupted his sentence: the sound of running, stumbling feet outside.

'Who's that?' began the inspector, and the words had scarcely left his lips when a scream split through the stillness of the dawn. It was a woman's scream, and ended as abruptly as it began.

'Good God!' gasped Tony, swinging round and facing the door. 'What the deuce was that?'

Jack went over to the window and flung it open, but Lowe was already out in the hall. Pushing aside the startled constable, he undid the latch of the front door and jerked it back.

At first he could see nothing, and then he caught sight of the crumpled heap that lay in the shadow of the porch. Whipping out his torch, he sent a white beam stabbing the greyness, and directed it fully upon the motionless form at his feet.

Lying quite still, her eyes closed and her fair hair in confusion, was a woman — the woman whom Lowe had seen at Monk's Lodge that afternoon.

5

A Fresh Development

Trevor Lowe, with the others grouped at his elbow, stood gazing down at the still-unconscious woman, who had been carried in and laid on the sofa in the sitting-room. The dramatist had made a hurried examination and assured himself that she was suffering from nothing more serious than a fainting fit. Lowe's expression was thoughtful as he waited for her to recover her senses. What had brought her there, and whence had come the shock that had caused her to faint? The scream she had uttered had been full of fear, even terror. What had she seen that had frightened her so?

'Who is the young lady, do any of you know?' inquired Inspector Jesson, looking round questioningly.

'Yes; she is staying at a cottage in Friar's Vale,' volunteered Jack. 'I don't know who she is, but we saw her the other day. She was with an elderly man, and I think they had just moved in.'

'I see.' The inspector nodded. 'That would be the people who've taken old Dinwood's place. Let me see now, I did hear their name. What was it?' He puckered up his forehead in an effort of memory, but at that moment the lips of the woman on the sofa moved slightly, and she sighed. Her head slipped to one side, and the long dark lashes of her eyes flickered. They saw a tinge of colour creep into the marble whiteness of her cheeks.

'She's coming round,' murmured Lowe with satisfaction. He took his flask from his pocket and held it to her lips, forcing a few drops of the potent spirit between her clenched teeth. After a lapse of a few seconds, she opened her eyes and stared up at Lowe through half-closed lids. Then, with a little cry of fear, she made a weak effort to push him away.

'Come now,' said the playwright kindly, 'there's nothing to be frightened about!'

Without heeding, the woman struggled into a sitting posture. Her large eyes were wide open now, but their blue depths were misty and vague. Quite suddenly the vacant expression faded as, with the return of full consciousness, memory came flooding back.

'Oh, I'm so frightened!' she murmured in a low voice, and glanced round swiftly.

'I can assure you that there is no need for any alarm,' said Lowe soothingly. 'You're in Monk's Lodge, and quite safe.'

She looked up at him and raised a shaking hand to her lips. 'I'm afraid I'm being very silly,' she said jerkily. 'I went to the police station first, but they told me the inspector was here.' She stopped with a little shiver, and again glanced swiftly behind her. 'Who — who was that man outside?' she whispered. 'I saw him just as I was going to knock at the door. He jumped away from the window at the side.'

'What was he doing at the window?' said Lowe.

'I don't know,' the woman answered. 'The bushes hid him. I didn't see him at all until he sprang out at me.'

'Did he try and attack you?' asked the dramatist.

She shook her head. 'No, no; it was his sudden appearance that frightened me

— and his eyes. There was just enough light to see, and — oh, it was horrible!' She closed her eyes as though to shut out the picture the memory had conjured up.

Inspector Jesson coughed and shifted his position, but before he could speak Lowe asked a question. 'What did the man look like?' he said.

'I didn't see him very clearly,' confessed the woman; 'but he had deep, rather piercing eyes set in a very white face, and a little black pointed beard.'

'By Jove, that's the fellow I saw looking through the hedge!' Tony Frost cried excitedly.

Ignoring Tony's interjection, the woman rose to her feet and clutched at Lowe's arm. 'You're wasting time,' she said quickly. 'While we are talking here, something terrible may be happening to Father!' She made a movement towards the door.

'Just a moment,' said the dramatist. 'You'd better tell us as quickly as possible what's happened. We know nothing yet. Why did you go to the police station, and what brought you up here at this hour of the morning?'

She made an effort to control her evident anxiety. 'I'm sorry,' she said. 'My name is Ursula Wyse, and I'll explain it all to you. I had been to bed for some time when I was awakened by a noise downstairs, as if somebody had stumbled over a chair. I looked at the clock beside my bed and saw that it was half-past three. I could hear someone moving about in the house, and I thought perhaps it was my father. I opened my door and called out, and immediately the noise stopped. I heard the sound of a window opening and whispering voices. I called out again, but there was no reply, and then I got frightened and ran to Father's room. I tried the handle, but it was locked; and although I knocked and shouted, he didn't take any notice.'

She paused breathlessly, then: 'There was a light inside — I could see it shining under the door — but I couldn't get any answer from Father, and I didn't know what to do. Then it occurred to me to go for the police. I scrambled into some clothes and ran all the way to the station; but when I got there, there was only a policeman in charge, and he said he couldn't leave, but I should find the inspector here. That's why I came.'

'We'll go along to your cottage at once,' said Lowe swiftly, 'but I don't think you should accompany us, Miss Wyse. Stay here with Mr. Denton until you feel stronger.'

She hesitated; but Jack, who thought this was one of the brightest notions that Lowe had yet conceived, added his urgings and eventually she consented.

'I'll come with you,' said Tony; and although the inspector looked dubious, Lowe accepted his suggestion before that official could demur.

Leaving Jack to look after Ursula Wyse, they set off in the grey light of the breaking day towards Friar's Vale, and in spite of their brisk pace, over half an hour had elapsed before they came in sight of the cottage. It was a small four-roomed building standing a little way from the road and partly concealed by the trees that grew around it. In one of the front upper windows a light was burning.

They found the front door of the place ajar. Pushing it open, Lowe entered, followed closely by Tony and the inspector.

The hall beyond merely consisted of a narrow passage, the walls of which were papered in a dull mustard colour, the design of which had long since vanished with age. There was an apology for a hat-stand, above which, at a drunken angle, hung a dusty and faded oleograph picture of Queen Victoria. Without pausing to appreciate these artistic decorations, Lowe pulled open a door on the right and then stopped dead on the threshold with an exclamation.

'Look at that!' he remarked, and Tony and the inspector peered into the room beyond over his shoulder.

It had apparently been used by the occupants as a sort of library-sitting-room, but at the moment it looked as if an earthquake had struck it! A bookcase had been ruthlessly flung open, and the books it had contained lay strewn in disordered confusion all over the floor. A small writing-desk in the corner had been forced open and its contents scattered about in every direction. Even the cushions of the two armchairs and the seats themselves had been ripped open and the stuffing dragged out.

Lowe swept his eyes round the room

quickly and then turned to the others. 'We can leave this until later,' he said curtly. 'The first thing to do is to find out what's happened to the woman's father.'

He closed the door, and they made their way up the narrow, dingy flight of stairs to a small and equally dingy landing. There were two doors on either side, but it was easy to distinguish the one they wanted, for a thin pencil of light shone out from beneath it.

The dramatist tried the handle. It was locked; and bending down, he applied his eye to the keyhole, but the view of the room he obtained was not extensive. All he could see was the foot of a bed and part of a dressing-table. He knocked loudly on the door, but there was no answer from inside.

'What do we do now?' said Inspector Jesson.

'We open the door,' said Lowe sharply; and stepping across, he took the key from the lock opposite. 'This key will probably fit. If it doesn't, we shall have to break in.'

The key did fit and, with a slight grating sound, the lock turned and Lowe pushed the door back. They looked in.

It was an ordinary bedroom, furnished

in rather an old-fashioned way. A paraffin lamp still burned on the dressing-table, the drawers of which had been pulled open and their contents turned out onto the floor. Next to the bed stood a chair with various articles of clothing on it. The four-poster bed, though it had been occupied, was now empty; and the clothes were thrown back, trailing half on the floor, as though the occupant had got up in a hurry. But the room was empty.

At least, that was Lowe's first impression. And then, as he took three steps forward, he saw that he had been mistaken.

In an armchair on the other side of the bed, and screened from the door by a hanging curtain, reclined a figure in pyjamas. It was that of an elderly man, with hair verging on silver. Around his face, so that it covered his mouth and nostrils, was a large white handkerchief, folded into the form of a pad.

The dramatist darted forward and bent over the occupant of the chair.

'Good God!' gasped Inspector Jesson. 'Is this another of 'em?'

Trevor Lowe removed the handkerchief and looked at the white face that was revealed. 'If you mean is he dead, then no,' he answered. 'But he is precious near it.'

'I say,' muttered Tony, sniffing loudly, 'there's a strange smell in here.'

Lowe straightened up and thrust the handkerchief into his hand. 'That's what you can smell,' he remarked grimly. 'It's been soaked with chloroform.'

6

The Clue of the Paint-flake

Mr. Wyse — for it was indeed he — could offer no explanation for the outrage at his cottage, when he recovered consciousness. He had awakened from a sound sleep to find the figure of a man at his bedside, but before he could cry out or utter any alarm the chloroformed pad had been pressed over his mouth. Although he had made an attempt to struggle against the fumes of the drug, it had overpowered him and robbed him of his senses.

He could suggest no reason, in spite of the repeated questions put to him by both Trevor Lowe and the inspector, why the unknown marauders should have turned the cottage upside down. He had nothing of any particular value there and was not in the habit of keeping any large sums of money in the house. His domestic bills were paid by cheque. He could only conclude that the whole matter was a very ordinary burglary and that the perpetrators had been so disappointed at finding nothing to reward them for their enterprise that they had wrecked the cottage in a sheer spirit of wilful damage.

To Lowe's suggestion that the appearance of the rooms seemed to indicate that the intruder or intruders had been searching for some particular object, Mr. Wyse replied with a vehement negative. So emphatic was he on this point that Lowe did not believe it. In fact, he did not believe Mr. Wyse's story at all.

His assertion that he had been chloroformed in bed before he had had time to give an alarm did not tally with the fact that they had found him in the armchair. Neither did it correspond with the state of the bed. The appearance of the clothes proved fairly conclusively to Lowe that Mr. Wyse had risen from that bed and had not been overpowered in it as he had stated; and if this was the case, he could not have been taken so much by surprise as he wished them to believe. And, therefore, he had had plenty of time to give an alarm if he had wanted to.

The dramatist, however, kept his suspicions to himself. There was no useful purpose to be served in letting the man see that he disbelieved his story, but he made a mental note that Mr. Wyse was worth a considerable amount of attention in the future, particularly when he remembered the behaviour of his daughter in the garden at Monk's Lodge when he had watched her from the window.

The whole manner of the man convinced Lowe that he was keeping something back. According to his story, he had come to Friar's Vale with Ursula because it was quiet and he was unlikely to be disturbed at his work. For Mr. Wyse revealed that he was a novelist, and one of that vast majority who turn out detective stories to satisfy the growing demand of an insatiable public. This may or may not have been true. A typewriter and a large stack of manuscript paper certainly served in some measure to bear out the truth of his words, and there was no doubt about his interest when he learned of the murder that had been committed at Monk's Lodge, and that no less a person than Trevor Lowe was mixed up in it. But still, author or not, Lowe was certain that Mr. Wyse had something to hide and that he was not all he appeared to be.

A search of the cottage by both Lowe and the inspector revealed no clue at all. The method by which the intruders had entered — the state of the place, and the fact that Ursula had said she had heard whisperings, seemed to point to more than one person being concerned — was through a small window at the back; a pane of glass had been neatly removed and the catch pulled back. There was a professional touch about this that showed that whoever was responsible were not amateurs at the job. So, also, did the fact that they had not left so much as a fingerprint behind them. On the glass of the bookcase Lowe found several smeared marks, but the hand that had made them had obviously been covered by a glove.

The sun was well up when they had finally completed their examination, and Lowe, leaving Inspector Jesson to return to the police station, walked back to Monk's

Lodge with Tony. The weary policeman on guard let them in, and they found Ursula and Jack drinking tea in the sitting-room.

In reply to Ursula's anxious questions, Lowe assured her that beyond a slight headache, her father was uninjured, and briefly related what they had found at the cottage. She seemed greatly relieved that it was nothing more serious; and, as in the case of Wyse himself, Lowe had an idea that she was keeping something back.

'By the way,' he said, accepting the cup of tea that Jack held out to him, with a nod of thanks, 'although you're unaware of it, we've met before.'

Her eyes widened in surprise. 'I don't remember,' she said hesitatingly.

'Oh, you didn't see me,' said Lowe with a smile. 'But I saw you — from the window, when you came to Monk's Lodge the other afternoon.'

Her rather pale face flushed, and she looked embarrassed. 'I — I didn't know there was anyone in. I'm afraid I was trespassing; but the garden looked so attractive from the road that I just had to come in.'

'What did you find in the flowerbed?'

remarked Lowe casually, sipping his tea.

The colour ebbed from her face. 'In — in — er — the flowerbed?' she repeated. 'Oh, yes, I remember what you mean,' she added quickly. 'I dropped my handkerchief.'

She was lying, and Lowe knew she was lying. It had not been a handkerchief she had picked up from that mass of tangled blossoms. The object, whatever it was, had been much smaller. He said nothing, however, accepting her explanation as though he believed it, and presently she rose and announced her intention of going home.

'I'll come with you,' said Jack hastily, and glared at Tony's sudden smile.

When they had gone, and declining Tony's offer of assistance, Lowe made his way upstairs to the lumber-room. Ogden's body still lay where they had first discovered it, for the ambulance had not yet arrived from Friar's Vale to convey it to the mortuary to await the inquest. The sun was streaming through the little window, flooding the room with light.

Shutting the door, the dramatist began a close and thorough examination. He had been unable to carry this out before with sufficient care to satisfy himself, for the dim light of the oil-lamp had been insufficient for his purpose. Now, however, every corner of the room was clearly visible. Starting from the door, he worked his way gradually over the entire apartment, moving the trunks and other odds and ends that it contained, and not even a speck of dust escaped his scrutiny.

It was not, however, until he reached the window and was looking at the frame that he discovered anything. And then, just below the catch and clearly visible in the grime that filmed the paintwork, was a distinct fingerprint. Taking out a penknife, the dramatist carefully slipped the thin steel blade between the paint and the woodwork, and by patient manipulation succeeded in removing a flake about the size of a two-shilling piece. It bore the impression that he wished to preserve; and, taking a small envelope from his pocket, he placed the paint-flake inside and licked down the flap. He found nothing else, although he searched carefully; and leaving the room, he went back again downstairs, where

Tony was engaged in cooking himself some breakfast.

'What time do they open the post office?' asked Lowe.

'Nine o'clock,' replied Tony, spearing a spluttering rasher of bacon with a fork and skilfully turning it.

Lowe glanced at his watch. It was a quarter-past eight. 'Then it will just be nine by the time I get there,' he said.

'Won't you have some breakfast first?' said Tony. 'It's just ready.'

The dramatist shook his head. 'Keep it hot in the oven until I come back,' he replied. 'I've got an important letter that I want to get off as soon as possible.'

It was just nine when he turned into the little shop. Buying some paper and envelopes, he scribbled a note, enclosed it together with the small envelope containing the paint-flake in one of the envelopes, addressed it to Detective-Inspector Shadgold, New Scotland Yard, London, and handed it to the old lady behind the counter with the request that it should be registered.

He was leaving the post office when he saw Inspector Jesson coming along on the opposite side of the street. The inspector saw him at the same time and crossed over.

'I've been on the phone to the chief constable,' Jesson said, 'and he's calling in the assistance of Scotland Yard. He's getting through to them at once, so I expect they'll be sending a man down later on today. It's a pity. I'd like to've had a go at this case myself. Only real chance I've ever 'ad, and now I suppose the Yard'll step in and collar all the credit.'

'I'll see that you get all the credit that's due to you, Inspector,' said Lowe, who was not without sympathy for the man.

'That's very good of you, sir,' Jesson said.

Lowe walked with him as far as the police station. When he got back to Monk's Lodge, he found that the ambulance had been during his absence, and that the remains of Mr. Ogden had been removed.

Nothing occurred during the morning, and both Jack and Tony, who appeared in very low spirits, whiled away the time by rambling about the garden.

Just after lunch a telegram arrived for Lowe. He read the brief message and thrust it into his pocket. 'Inspector Shadgold is coming down this afternoon,' he said. 'He arrives at King's Hayling just after four. Do you think we could manage to put him up here? I'd rather like to have him with us if it is possible.'

'Of course! Bring him along,' said Jack, and Tony nodded his agreement.

Lowe walked into King's Hayling, partly because he enjoyed the exercise, but mostly because it was the only way of getting there. Shadgold arrived by the same train that he had come on himself. He was a big, large-boned, heavily built man, red of face and cheery.

'Hello, Mr. Lowe!' he said as he shook hands. 'Now what's all this business? I've only got the barest outline. The chief constable rang up the Yard this morning, and they put me on to the case, but they couldn't give me much information — said that I could get all there was to be had when I arrived.'

'Before I answer any of your questions,' said Lowe, 'I want to ask you one. How did you know that I was down here?'

Shadgold grinned. 'Happened to drop in and see Mr. White yesterday, and he told me,' he replied. 'He was grumbling because the repairs to your car kept him from joining you. When they told me about this job, I remembered you were staying at the same place, so I wired you.'

As they came out of the railway station, the dramatist, who had no particular wish to walk the six miles back to Monk's Lodge if it could be avoided, looked round in the hope of finding the car that Jack and Tony had hired on the day that he had arrived. There was no sign of it, and he questioned a woman selling papers. She shook her head decisively.

'No, sir, no moty-car ever stan' 'ere.'

'Surely you're mistaken,' said Lowe. 'I myself was taken to Friar's Vale in it only a few days ago.'

But the woman was positive. 'Then it 'appened to be 'ere just that day,' she asserted. 'It's never bin 'ere before, and it's never bin 'ere since. I'll take my oath on that, and I ought to know, seeing as 'ow I'm 'ere regular every day of me life.'

Lowe was very thoughtful as he moved away. 'Now that's very odd,' he muttered, partly to himself; 'very odd indeed.'

'What's odd?' asked the burly inspector in surprise.

'What that woman said,' replied the dramatist.

'I don't see anything odd about it,' argued Shadgold.

'You will when you hear the whole story,' said Lowe, and he proceeded to tell Shadgold as they walked towards Monk's Lodge.

7

The Monk

They had almost reached Monk's Lodge by the time Lowe had finished giving Shadgold a detailed account of what had happened. The inspector listened in silence until the dramatist had come to the end of his story.

'It's a funny business,' he said then. 'I suppose all these episodes have a connection, but I'm hanged if I can see it at the moment. There doesn't appear to have been any motive for Ogden's murder at all.'

'But there *is* a motive somewhere, and a very strong motive,' replied Lowe. 'In my opinion Ogden was killed because he was unfortunate enough to know something concerning Monk's Lodge, and the killer was afraid that he was going to pass that knowledge on.'

'What knowledge could Ogden have had?' asked Shadgold.

'I haven't the least idea,' Lowe said.

'That's one of the things that we have to discover. If we knew that, there wouldn't be any mystery.'

The burly inspector frowned. 'If it's your belief,' he said, 'that Ogden was killed outside — and from what you tell me about the marks on his clothes, I'm inclined to agree with you — why should the body have been placed in the lumber-room at all? Why didn't the killer leave it in the place where the crime was committed?'

'Well, it seems to me fairly obvious that some person or persons, for reasons of their own, are trying to get Monk's Lodge to themselves,' Lowe said. 'In other words, they want Denton and Frost out of it — out of the way. That's the only possible explanation of the warning that was written on the window. Now that warning failed in its effect; and when it became necessary to remove Ogden, because he was on the point of saying something that would put these people in danger, they concealed the body in the locked room with the sole intention of directing suspicion on Denton and Frost, hoping that this would achieve what the melodramatic warning had failed to do.'

Shadgold nodded his bullet head quickly. 'That's quite a logical piece of reasoning, Mr. Lowe,' he agreed. 'But how did they get the body into the house without being seen? Surely it was an enormous risk to run?'

The dramatist smiled. 'You forget,' he pointed out, 'that Denton and Frost are on holiday, so they are out most of the day for hours on end, and Monk's Lodge is a very lonely spot. It hasn't got a very good reputation in the village, there's a lot of stupid nonsense about it being haunted by the phantom of a monk or some such person — the local name for it is Phantom Hollow — and nobody goes near it, apparently, if they can possibly help it.'

'I see,' muttered the inspector. 'That sounds logical. I suppose you haven't any idea where the crime was actually committed?'

'No — except that it must have been quite close to the cottage,' Lowe replied, and Shadgold looked at him quickly.

'What makes you think that?' he asked.

'The warning on the window,' said the dramatist quietly.

'Good God!' Shadgold cried, a note of

horror in his voice. 'You don't mean —'

'I mean that that warning on the window was written with Ogden's blood,' Lowe finished grimly, and for the rest of the short distance that separated them from Monk's Lodge Detective-Inspector Shadgold was a very silent and thoughtful man.

Jack and Tony were in the midst of tea; and to the inspector's concealed annoyance — for he was hoping to have had a chance of questioning them concerning the strange business which had brought him down — they were not alone. A rather pretty woman was seated beside the teapot, and near her an elderly grey-haired man. Shadgold recognised them both from Lowe's description. They must be Wyse and his daughter, whom Lowe had mentioned, and who seemed to be deeply involved in the mysterious affair. His supposition was confirmed when Jack introduced them.

'It has always been a wish of mine,' said Mr. Wyse, passing his cup to Ursula to be refilled, 'to meet a detective-inspector from Scotland Yard in the flesh. I've written about these people over and over again, but this is the first time that I've had the pleasure of meeting one.'

'I hope you're not disappointed,' said Shadgold. 'I understand that you're a criminologist, Mr. Wyse?'

'Hardly,' Wyse said, waving his head deprecatingly. 'A mere scribbler of sensational literature, Inspector.'

'I'm afraid I haven't had the pleasure of reading any of your books,' said Lowe.

'In that respect,' Wyse said, shaking his head sadly, 'I'm sorry to say that you are in common with a great many other people. My manuscripts have so far not seen the light of day. Although I have submitted them to various publishers, I regret to say that they have not deemed them worthy of print. However —' He sighed resignedly. '—I shall continue to write them if only for my own pleasure. My work is a labour of love, Mr. Lowe. You, of course, being a writer yourself, will appreciate that.'

Shadgold listened to this speech with a faint trace of bewilderment, and came to the conclusion that Mr. Wyse was slightly touched.

'I'm immensely interested,' the author continued, leaning back in his chair, 'in everything appertaining to crime. I think I may say without boasting that my library on the subject is one of the completest in the world.' He paused and looked across at the dramatist. 'Tell me, Mr. Lowe,' he said, 'have you made any fresh discoveries in connection with this terrible business that has happened in our midst?'

'No, I am afraid I haven't,' Lowe replied, slowly stirring the contents of his cup. 'I don't pretend to be a detective, Mr. Wyse. I am merely a student of human nature and human motives, and these I sift and sift, till all the dust has passed away and only the stones of importance remain.'

'Very well put — very well put, indeed!' remarked Mr. Wyse, nodding his silver head. 'Really, I must remember that, and include it in one of my stories. But surely you have some theory with regard to this crime?'

'To be perfectly candid I have six,' replied Lowe. 'But I'm afraid at the present juncture you must excuse me from discussing them.'

'I quite understand — very proper!' Wyse said, and changed the subject.

The conversation reverted to that disjointed small talk which usually occurs when several people are gathered together. When dusk had fallen and Shadgold and Lowe were beginning to think that Mr. Wyse was never going, that gentleman rose reluctantly and announced that they must be returning home.

'I'll walk with you if you have no objection,' said Jack quickly. 'I want some stamps.'

Tony grinned. It was the flimsiest of excuses, because he happened to know that Jack had a nearly full book of stamps upstairs in the bedroom.

'If you're going to the post office,' he drawled, 'you might post this letter to the guv'nor for me.'

Jack took it and slipped it into his pocket. Outside the Wyses' cottage he said goodbye to them; and if he held Ursula's hand a trifle longer than was strictly necessary, there was certainly every excuse, for she was the type that is often seen on the covers of magazines but seldom in the flesh.

It was nearly dark by the time Jack had posted Tony's letter and started on his return journey. The night was fine, with a silvery moon, and he decided that instead of following the usual route to Monk's Lodge, he would cut across the fields and take the path through the wood. It was a little further that way, but Jack was in no special need to hurry, and it offered a pleasant change.

As he trudged along over the rough ground, his mind was a trifle chaotic. Ursula was the main subject of his thoughts; but as a kind of sub-stratum, the murder and the curious incidents that had led up to it kept on breaking through. It was all very queer, and the queerest to Jack's mind was how Ursula fitted into the tangle. She was in it somehow, but whatever part she was playing, he was convinced that it was a perfectly innocent one. It would be impossible for a woman with a face like that to do anything else.

One thing seemed pretty certain — someone was mighty anxious to get Tony and himself out of Monk's Lodge. But why? The peculiar behaviour of the postmistress and the stories of Monk's Lodge being haunted rose unbidden to his mind. Sheer

90

nonsense, of course! These uneducated villagers believed in such illogical things.

But *was* it nonsense? After all, some men of science believed in supernatural phenomena. There were more things in heaven and earth than the mind of man dreamed of, and however absurd they might appear in broad daylight, with the hush of the falling night and the ghostly light of the moon casting long shadows across his path, Jack began to feel that perhaps they were not quite so absurd as he had imagined.

It was curious that Mr. Ogden, a practical man of business, should have considered them of sufficient importance to warrant a warning. But had it been his intention to warn them about the stories concerning Monk's Lodge? Jack realised that no other explanation seemed feasible in the circumstances, but at the same time it was not definite, because poor Ogden had never been able to keep his appointment.

He had reached the fringe of the wood that flanked Monk's Lodge; and as he continued his way along the almost invisible path, the utter stillness seemed to wrap him like a blanket. The trees and their merging shadows took on a movement of their own; and high up, stirred by the faint breeze, the branches rustled softly every now and again, not breaking that peculiar silence, but curiously, as it seemed to Jack, accentuating it and becoming part of it. It was as if they resented his intrusion into the privacy of their domain, and were whispering little warnings to one another.

It was soft and mossy underfoot, and Jack's advance was noiseless; so silent that he did not disturb a rabbit that was directly in his path until he had almost trodden on it. It scampered away into the undergrowth, and in spite of himself Jack's heart beat a little faster, for the sudden movement of the animal had given him something of a shock.

'I must say, that this place is enough to give anyone the creeps,' he muttered. 'I almost wish I'd come the other way now.'

He had not far to go now, however. Another three minutes would see him through the wood and out by the gate of the cottage. He was feeling in his pocket for his cigarette case when a sound to his right, somewhere among the clustered tree trunks, brought him to a dead stop.

The sound was repeated: soft swishing noise, like the trailing of some garment over the undergrowth.

Jack stared into the blackness, but he could see nothing. Then, just as he was about to move on again, having convinced himself that the noise he had heard was made by some animal, a shadow moved among the trees! Unconsciously holding his breath, Jack watched it. A little way ahead was a break in the trees through which the pale light of the moon filtered, forming a circle of radiance on the ground; and as he watched, a figure came out of the darkness and crossed this little patch of light. He caught a momentary glimpse of the long gown and the hood in which it was dressed, and then it vanished into the shadows once more.

Jack was not lacking in courage, and would have faced anything human, but he was convinced that the thing he had seen was not human. The stories of the phantom monk that haunted Monk's Lodge were true — the villagers were right; and in a sudden panic he turned and crashed through the undergrowth. Not for a fortune would he have passed the spot where the horrible thing had vanished!

Before he fully realised it, he had burst, torn and bleeding, from the cover of the wood and was forcing his way through the straggling hedge that divided the garden of Monk's Lodge. And then two strong hands gripped him by the shoulders.

'What's the matter, Denton? What happened?' exclaimed the voice of Trevor Lowe.

Jack gasped with the sudden relief. Breathlessly and disjointedly, he related what he had seen.

'Get indoors!' snapped the dramatist crisply, and before Jack could reply he had disappeared into the darkness.

Picking his way through the undergrowth, so that while he moved swiftly his progress was practically silent, Lowe went on until he came to the little clearing in the wood where Jack had seen the cowled figure. Here he paused and took an electric torch from his pocket. He did not press the button, but remained motionless, listening intently. Then somewhere to his left he heard the soft pad, pad of footsteps on the mossy ground.

A dim figure appeared among the trees,

and Lowe moved cautiously forward. Unfortunately, however, when he was within five yards of his quarry he trod on a dead branch, the wood snapped with a sharp crack, and the figure in front looked round swiftly.

Lowe broke into a run, for concealment was now useless, but the other had also taken alarm and went racing away as hard as they could. But whoever it was, the fugitive was no match for the dramatist. Putting on an extra spurt, Lowe leapt forward and, catching his quarry by the arm, jerked them round. The stranger fought like a tiger, but eventually Lowe succeeded in getting the upper hand; and, sitting astride his captive, he pinned them to the ground.

'Now then, my friend,' he panted, 'let's have a look at you!'

He heard a gasp as he dragged the torch from his pocket, where he had put it when he began the chase; and pressing the button, he directed the light full on the face and form of the person he was holding. He uttered an exclamation of amazement.

It was Dr. MacGuire, the divisional surgeon!

8

Information from the Yard

The prostrate man glared up at Trevor Lowe, blinking in the light of the torch. 'Perhaps you'll kindly explain,' he panted, 'what this unwarrantable outrage means?'

The dramatist rose to his feet and assisted the divisional surgeon to a more dignified position. 'What are you doing here?' he asked sharply.

'Really, sir,' McGuire retorted, 'I cannot see that that's any business of yours! The kindest way I can account for your atrocious conduct is to presume that you've suddenly taken leave of your senses.'

Lowe eyed the angry man keenly. Had he made a mistake after all? The doctor was wearing an ordinary suit of clothes; there was no sign of the monk's habit which Jack Denton had described. 'Have you seen anyone else near here?' he asked.

'I've seen nobody,' snarled Dr. McGuire,

brushing his clothes vigorously. 'I don't know what you're talking about. I go to see a patient and decide to take a short cut home through these woods. On the way I'm viciously attacked for no apparent reason at all. I certainly think that instead of putting a lot of ridiculous questions to me, it would be better if you offered some sort of an explanation and apology.'

Before the dramatist could reply, there came the sound of running footsteps, and a moment later Jack Denton and Inspector Shadgold joined them. 'What's the matter here, Mr. Lowe?' panted the latter. 'Have you got him?'

'I'm afraid there's been a slight mistake,' replied Lowe. 'I mistook Dr. McGuire for the man Denton saw.'

The divisional surgeon grunted. 'Perhaps you wouldn't mind telling me what all this foolery is about?' he said curtly.

Jack briefly related his recent experience, and when he had finished the doctor sniffed. 'I don't think that's any excuse for the way I've been treated,' he grumbled. 'Do I look like the — er — whatever it was Mr. Denton saw, or imagined he saw?'

The dramatist admitted that he did not, but his brain was working rapidly. Had he made a mistake in the dim shadows of the wood? It was quite possible. He had only caught the vaguest glimpse of the divisional surgeon, a mere blur of moving blackness. On the other hand, there was nothing to have prevented McGuire from discarding the monk's robe and hiding it somewhere in the wood. Lowe knew he could not, however, openly accuse the doctor of having done this. The man might, after all, be speaking the truth.

'It seems that there's been a misunderstanding, Dr. McGuire,' he apologised, having decided to take a diplomatic approach, 'and I can only say that I'm sorry for having attacked you. I'm sure, however, that if you consider the matter, you'll realise there was a reason for my actions.'

'Perhaps there was,' the doctor said grudgingly. 'Now do you mind turning that light of yours onto the ground and seeing if you can find my glasses anywhere? I've lost the confounded things thanks to you, and I'm as blind as a bat without them.'

The dramatist acceded to the request,

and they all joined in the search. It was Jack who found them a few yards away in a patch of undergrowth.

Dr. McGuire took them with a grunt, polished them on his handkerchief, and adjusted them on the bridge of his thin nose. Carefully brushing his soft hat with his coat-sleeve, he jammed them on his head and turned to Lowe. 'Well, I can't waste any more time here,' he said. 'Good night, and in future be a little more careful.'

They watched him until he had disappeared into the darkness.

'Surly sort of fellow,' muttered Shadgold. 'Who is he?'

Lowe explained.

'Hmm!' grunted the Scotland Yard man. 'Shouldn't like to be one of his patients!' He turned to Jack. 'Where did you see this fellow dressed as a monk?'

Jack pointed to the moon-illumined clearing. 'He came out of the shadows on the right,' he answered, 'crossed that open space, and disappeared into the undergrowth on the other side.'

'Whoever he is, he's probably miles away by now,' said the dramatist; 'but since we're here, we may as well look and see if he's left any traces.'

They followed him towards the little straggling patch of moonlight, and Lowe examined the bushes into which the figure had vanished. 'There was nothing supernatural about him, anyway,' he said after a second or two. He pointed to several broken branches and twigs. 'Solid flesh and blood did that. There's no question that someone forced their way through here recently.' He leaned forward suddenly and detached something from a large thorn. 'This proves that you weren't imagining things,' he said to Jack, and held the object out in the palm of his hand.

Shadgold and Jack peered at it in the light of Lowe's torch. It was a small strip of black material — a rather coarse serge — and it had obviously been ripped from some garment.

'That came from the robe that our friend was wearing,' said the playwright; and he slipped it into his pocket.

'What's the object of all this tomfoolery?' Shadgold demanded. 'What's the idea of wandering about masquerading as a monk?'

Lowe shrugged. 'No doubt because he wishes to be able to move about Monk's Lodge without fear of being molested,' he answered. 'There's a local superstition that the place is haunted, and one of the stories concerns the ghost of a monk who is supposed to appear now and again. It's based, of course, on the fact that Monk's Lodge is the site of an old monastery. Anybody who wanted to prowl about the place without risk of being challenged couldn't have adopted a better idea. There's not a solitary soul in the village who wouldn't run for miles at the first glimpse of him.'

They walked back to the cottage, each man occupied with his own thoughts. Lowe was wondering whether Dr. McGuire was, after all, connected with this strange business. Shadgold was mentally going over all the facts that he had learnt that day, while Jack was chiefly concerned with what a certain slim, fair-haired woman might be doing at that particular moment.

Tony Frost had just finished preparing the supper when they got back, and was intensely curious to hear the latest development. Only the risk of spoiling the omelette had prevented him from coming out with Jack and Shadgold himself.

'I shouldn't be surprised if it was the doctor chappy,' he remarked. 'I didn't like his face or anything about him. A most objectionable fellow.'

'You may quite possibly be right,' replied Lowe. 'But you can't accuse a man of being mixed up with a serious crime because you don't like his face. We ought to get a reply to my letter tomorrow,' he added, looking across at Shadgold.

The inspector nodded. 'May prove a disappointment,' he said, reaching for the pepper. 'There may be nothing to correspond with that print in Records.'

Jack and Tony looked interested, for the dramatist had made no mention of the fingerprint he had found on the paintwork of the lumber-room window. But their curiosity was not satisfied, for nothing more was said about it, and shortly after supper they all went to bed.

Shadgold left early on the following morning to call on the chief constable at King's Hayling, and to have an interview with Inspector Jesson.

It had been arranged after the discovery of Ogden's body that the cottage should never be left completely empty; that one or other of the little party should remain behind as a sort of guard. Since Lowe had no particular plans for that morning, he elected this duty for himself.

Jack and Tony went off to the village for further supplies, and during their absence Lowe rambled about the house and garden, smoking and thinking, and trying to evolve some theory that would reasonably cover the series of strange incidents that had culminated in the murder of the estate agent. But, try as he would, the dramatist could not construct any workable hypothesis. Beyond the actual murder, there was nothing tangible. Something unknown was happening in and around that peaceful and beautiful spot.

Jack and Tony came home for lunch, and after the meal the former tried to persuade Lowe to accompany him over to Dryseley, but the playwright was in no mood for exercise. The problem surrounding Monk's Lodge was worrying him, so Tony went instead.

It was late in the afternoon before Inspector Shadgold returned, looking hot and tired and dusty. That he had contrived to pick up some news of interest Lowe guessed after one glance at his flushed and perspiring face.

'Jove,' said the burly inspector, flopping into a chair and producing a large handkerchief, 'I shouldn't like to live long in this neighbourhood. You've got to walk miles before you get anywhere.' He mopped his forehead vigorously. 'Anyway, I've discovered something peculiar.' He took the cup of tea that Lowe poured out for him and gulped the steaming fluid with evident enjoyment.

'Tell me all about it,' said the dramatist.

'Well, I saw the chief constable,' began Shadgold, 'had a chat with him, and then went over to Dryseley to see what I could pick up regarding Ogden. He seems to have been a steady, fairly quiet fellow, and I didn't learn anything that suggested even the ghost of a motive for anybody wanting to murder him. The course of my inquiries, however, led me to the post office; and one of the telegraph-boys whom I was questioning about Ogden — I wanted to know if he'd received any telegrams — told me a curious story. It appears that a few days ago he was bringing a telegram up here when his bicycle got a puncture. He was just going to set to work and mend it when a stranger came up to him — a queer-looking fellow, he says, with a little black beard. On learning that the boy was on his way to Monk's Lodge, he said that he was going that way, and offered to take the wire himself.'

'Did the boy say who the wire was addressed to?' Lowe asked sharply.

'Yes, young Frost,' Shadgold replied.

'It must have been the wire that White sent with the time of my arrival,' muttered the dramatist. 'You cleared up one point, Shadgold, which has been bothering me a lot. I wondered how they got the information that enabled them to plan that attempt on my life. It's easy to understand now why that car was waiting at the station, and apparently had never been seen there before. They knew the train I was coming on, guessed that Denton and Frost would want some sort of conveyance to bring me back to Monk's Lodge, and planned the whole thing.'

'Yes,' said Shadgold. 'The same thing occurred to me when I heard the lad's story. It seems that when he heard about the murder he thought it was his duty to tell the police about this incident of the telegram, but he didn't like to because he was scared of losing his job. There's only one thing I can't quite understand. The driver of the car didn't have a beard, did he?'

Lowe shook his head. 'No,' he answered. 'It must have been the man with the beard who used the rifle, and that shows us we've got at least two people to deal with.'

The inspector grunted. 'I'd like to know what the game is.'

'So would I,' admitted Lowe. 'There's —'

He broke off as there came a knock on the front door. Leaving the sitting-room, he crossed the tiny hall and opened it.

'Name of Lowe?' said the aged postman.

'That's right,' said the dramatist, and he took the letter the other held out in a gnarled hand.

Carrying it back to the room he had left, he opened it, with a word of apology to

Shadgold. It was from Scotland Yard, and as he glanced at the contents his eyes glinted and his face went tense. 'Listen, Shadgold,' he said, speaking rapidly, 'this is in answer to the letter I sent asking for information about that fingerprint.' He read aloud an extract from the letter: 'Specimen of print sent corresponds with the right index finger of a man named Joseph Luckman. This man was convicted for the murder of a night watchman on the premises of Messrs. Gilbert, Lane & Co., diamond merchants of Hatton Gardens, four years ago. Medical evidence was, however, brought forward by the defence to prove that he was insane, and he was sent to Broadmoor criminal asylum for a life sentence.'

'By Jove!' exclaimed Shadgold, jumping up from his chair excitedly. 'I remember the case well. He got away with a hundred thousand pounds' worth of diamonds, which he chucked in the Thames before he was arrested. But if he's in Broadmoor, how the deuce did his fingerprint get here?'

'If you'll let me finish, you'll see,' said Lowe. He continued reading: 'Luckman escaped from Broadmoor three weeks ago, and is still at large. We shall be glad to have any information that may supply a clue to his whereabouts.' Lowe folded the report and put it in his pocket, looking across at the Scotland Yard man in silence. 'I think this helps us take a step forward,' he said, at length. 'At least we know who we've got to look for.'

'Joseph Luckman,' Shadgold breathed softly. 'The insane murderer.'

'Not so insane as they made out,' retorted Lowe. 'I was intensely interested in the case, and through a friend on the Press I managed to get a ticket for the Old Bailey. If ever a man ought to have been hanged, Luckman was that man. The murder was a particularly brutal one; the watchman was scarcely recognisable when they found him. Of course, Luckman had a kink — but then, so have all criminals. But insane, as the average person understands the word, he was not. He was merely abnormal.'

'Insane or not, he appears to be loose somewhere in this district,' said Shadgold, 'and we've got to find him.'

9

The Men in the Night

The man who was watching from the shadow of the wood moved his cramped limbs and stifled a yawn. The vigil had been a long one. For over two hours he had lain concealed among the thick undergrowth with his piercing little black eyes fixed on the lighted windows of Monk's Lodge.

Presently he saw the window of the sitting-room darken, and after a little while lights appeared in two of the upstairs rooms. These, too, went out after an interval, and the cottage became wrapped in darkness. But the watcher still remained where he was.

Another hour dragged slowly by, and then he cautiously wriggled his way from the screen of foliage that had covered him and rose stealthily to his feet. The mournful hoot of an owl broke the silence of the night, and so skilful was the imitation that it was scarcely possible to believe that it had emanated from the stranger's bearded lips.

Twice he repeated the call, and then waited in silence, listening intently. The faint sound of rustling leaves and crunching twigs reached his ears after several minutes, and his eyes, which had grown accustomed to the darkness, made out the faint blot of shadow that indicated the figure of his approaching companion. The man who had driven the car from Friar's Vale to Monk's Lodge on the day that Lowe arrived from London drew level with the other, and laid down a bulky parcel he was carrying with a sigh of relief.

'That's heavy,' he whispered. 'I was beginning to think that we should have to wait all night. Everything O.K.?'

The bearded man nodded. 'Yes,' he said, speaking in the same low tone. 'They're all gone to bed, and I've given them an hour to get thoroughly asleep. Bring that stuff and follow me, and be as quiet as you can.'

'Which is the room?' breathed the other as he stooped to pick up his parcel.

'I'll tell you when we get to the cottage,' was the reply. 'Keep close to the hedge, and don't show yourself in the open. Once we're under the walls of the place itself, we're pretty safe. I don't suppose there's anybody awake, but I don't want to take any chances.'

They crept forward through the darkness, and, emerging from the wood, skirted the straggling hedge that bordered the garden of Monk's Lodge. At the foot of the south wall of the cottage they stopped, and the man with the beard unwrapped a coil of some flexible material which he had worn wound around his waist underneath his coat. He handed the end of this to his companion without a word. While the other was engaged in fixing it to a long, narrow, oblong object that formed part of the parcel he had been carrying, the bearded man proceeded to fit together the joints of a long fishing rod. No word was uttered while they completed their preparations. The other end of the flexible tubing was fastened through a screw-ring at the top of the fishing rod. Slowly the rod, with the trailing rubber tubing attached, was raised until it was level with the windowsill above them. The window was half-open; and as the rod was pushed another six inches, the projecting end of the rubber pipe protruded into the room beyond.

The bearded man signalled to his companion, and a second later the stillness of the night was broken by a faint hissing sound. For nearly half an hour they remained motionless, the bearded man holding the fishing rod and his companion gently turning the stop-cock of the gas cylinder as the pressure decreased.

'I think that'll do now,' whispered the man with the beard, and he began cautiously to lower the rod.

The rubber tubing was removed, and its place taken by the hooks of a rope ladder. When these had been lodged firmly on the windowsill and the ladder tested, the bearded man fastened a respirator over his mouth and began to ascend the frail, swaying structure. Gently raising the window to its fullest extent, he climbed into the room. The sound of heavy breathing reached his ears; and, tiptoeing across to the bed, he bent down over the recumbent figure lying there. For perhaps half a minute he remained thus; then, apparently satisfied, he took an electric torch from his pocket and pressed the button. The light that came from it was very dim, for over the lens at the top had been stuck a piece of tissue paper, but it was sufficient for his purpose. Directing it full on the upturned face of Trevor Lowe, he raised the dramatist's eyelids. There was no sign of movement. The gas had obviously done its work. Replacing the torch in his pocket, he jerked back the bed-clothes and, picking up the unconscious figure of the dramatist, carried him to the window. Hoisting him over the sill, he dropped him into the arms of his waiting companion, and swiftly descended the ladder. A sharp jerk freed the hooks, and rolling it up, he stuffed it into his pocket.

Swiftly and noiselessly the fishing rod was taken to pieces and packed up together with the rubber tubing and the gas cylinder. Leaving his companion to look after the parcel, the bearded man swung the limp form of the unconscious dramatist across his shoulders fireman-fashion. They retraced their steps, and presently in the centre of the wood the bearded man put down his burden and wiped his streaming face.

'Very neatly done,' he whispered breathlessly. 'Hide all that stuff somewhere while I bind him.' He secured Lowe's wrists and ankles with a thin cord while the other man deposited the empty gas cylinder and the rest of the paraphernalia in the midst of a dense thicket.

'Now give me a hand,' said the man with the beard, 'and we'll finish the job. We shan't have anything to fear from Mr. Trevor-confounded-Lowe after tonight!'

They picked up the dramatist between them and set off in the direction of the river. Once, as they were nearing their destination, the man who had driven the car raised his head sharply and stopped. 'Did you hear anything?' he asked.

The other man strained his ears, but the night was perfectly still and silent. 'No; what was it?' muttered the other. 'I can't hear a sound.'

'I thought I heard something moving behind us,' replied his companion.

'Must have been a rabbit,' grunted the bearded man. He stopped and listened, all the same, for nearly half a minute before they continued their stumbling progress down the rough slope towards the river. Reaching the waterside, they paused.

'Now then, in with him!' said the bearded man harshly.

They gave the motionless form between them a forward heave and let go. There was a second's silence, and then a loud splash from the dark waters below.

'Come on!' murmured the bearded man, grasping the other by the arm. 'Let's get away!'

Without a backward glance, they took to their heels and disappeared into the blackness of the night.

★ ★ ★

With a deep and rhythmical throb of its high-powered engine, the big car turned slowly into the dark and deserted High Street of Dryseley, the blazing headlights throwing a penetrating white beam.

'Can't miss it, sir, if you keep on,' directed the policeman with a friendly salute as he stepped back to the pavement.

'Thanks,' replied White. With a smile and a nod at the obliging constable, he dexterously swung the car round and pressed his foot on the accelerator. The throbbing purr developed into a throaty roar, and the Rolls went smoothly forward into the blackness of the night.

He was feeling a trifle fed up, for when he had started from London that afternoon he had calculated on reaching his destination somewhere round ten o'clock. A breakdown on the road, however, had caused a long delay at Yeovil while it was being put right, with the result that it was now considerably after two. He had not the faintest idea of the exact location of Monk's Lodge, and had stopped at Dryseley to ask the policeman on night duty his way.

He slowed to take a bend, and then once more let the car have its head. Almost before he realised it, he found himself shooting past a collection of squat cottages, scattered and straggling.

'This must be Friar's Vale,' he muttered, and a little further on he came to a fork where two roads branched away to left and right.

White applied the brakes, and brought the car almost to a standstill. 'Now which of these goes to Monk's Lodge?' he said to himself. Getting out of the driver's seat, he went in search of a signpost. But if there had ever been such a thing, it was not there now.

'I suppose I shall have to risk it,' he thought disgustedly. 'I bet whichever road I take, it will be the wrong one!'

He was turning to walk back to the car when he saw a dim light among the trees to his left. It came from the downstairs window of a small cottage two or three hundred yards further on.

White took his place again behind the wheel and sent the car moving slowly forward towards the light. As it was in one of the lower rooms, it appeared to indicate that there was somebody still up, and there would be no harm in knocking and making sure of his direction.

Leaving the engine still running, he once more got out of the car, and, opening a little rustic gate, went up to the door and knocked gently. He heard the squeak of a chair pushed back, and then silence. Just as he was on the point of knocking again, however, there came a shuffling sound from within. A bolt was shot back with a rattle, and the door jerked open.

'Put up your hands!' said a voice grimly, and White found himself looking into a muzzle of a revolver. It was held by a tall man in his shirt-sleeves, whose silver hair gleamed in the light that streamed through an open door behind him.

'Put that thing away — it's all right,' said White hastily.

At the sound of his voice, the man lowered the weapon and peered at him closely. 'What do you want?' he irritably demanded.

White explained, and immediately the other's manner changed. 'I must apologise for my reception,' he said, smiling; 'only I've had burglars here recently, and therefore I was a little apprehensive of visitors at this hour. If you continue straight up this road, you'll come to a lane on your right. It's a little over three miles from here. You can't possibly miss it.'

'Thanks very much,' said White.

'Not at all — not at all!' said the man with a smile. 'I know them all up at Monk's Lodge quite well. My name is Wyse. I'm only too glad to have been able to help you.

By the way, I'm afraid the lane is too narrow for a car. It's really only a footpath.'

'I don't suppose there's much traffic along this road,' said White, 'so if I leave the car close up by the side, will it be all right until the morning?'

Mr. Wyse nodded. 'I should think, quite,' he replied. Shaking White warmly by the hand as he took his leave, he stood watching him until the car had moved away.

White had no difficulty in finding the lane, and one glance assured him that Mr. Wyse had not exaggerated when he had expressed his belief that it was too narrow for a car. It was barely four feet wide, and the thick hedges on either side almost met in places. He left the car close in by the edge of the road, taking the precaution to leave the rear and side lights burning, and set off up the lane to Monk's Lodge.

The sky was a bit cloudy, but every now and again there was sufficient light from the moon to enable him to see ahead. After he had been walking for a little while, he caught a glimpse of the cottage through a thin belt of trees. 'Nearly there,' he muttered with a sigh of satisfaction. 'Hope there's something to eat in the house. I'm starving!'

The geography of the lane had changed. The unkempt hedgerow still bordered it on the right-hand side, but to the left the ground sloped away to a dense wooded fastness that was impenetrable, in this light, from the roadway. The winding path was pretty steep here, and White paused for a moment to remove a stone that had slipped inside his shoe. As he straightened up from performing this task, he thought he saw a movement on the fringe of the wood at the bottom of the slope. He looked more closely, and just then the moon shone for a fitful second before being again obliterated by the passing clouds. But that second had been sufficient to enable him to see vaguely what it was that had attracted his attention: two figures were on the point of entering the wood, carrying something between them. White was determined to find out what they were doing at that hour and what it was they were carrying. There was something so furtive about their movements that he was convinced they were up to no good.

He slipped down the slope towards the

dark mass of trees, making his way rapidly but noiselessly towards the point where the men had been swallowed up in the darkness. Once he nearly gave himself away: his foot caught a stone and nearly sent him sprawling. He could hear the men he was following now making their way through the wood, and presently as the trees began to thin out he caught his second glimpse of them. They had come to a halt; and as White dodged behind a tree, watching them, he heard from somewhere ahead the faint lap-lap of water. There was a pause, broken by a murmuring of voices, and then a dull, heavy splash. The next moment the two men were hurrying away as fast as they could go, but they were no longer carrying their burden.

His heart throbbing with excitement, White left his hiding-place and ran down to the water's edge. The dark, swirling surface of the river looked cold and repellent as he peered in to see if he could catch a glimpse of the thing they had thrown in. And then he saw it!

Drifting out into mid-stream was a dark form almost completely submerged but for the dim white face. Without hesitation White ripped off his jacket and, taking a deep breath, dived cleanly, entering the water with scarcely a sound. A few strokes and he was beside that vague white thing that was even then disappearing beneath the surface.

Grasping the figure under the arms, he swam back to the bank and, scrambling out of the water, dragged the limp form onto dry land. Only then did he see who it was he had rescued, for the face that looked up at him was that of Trevor Lowe!

10

The Man in the Post Office

Except for a slight headache due to the after-effects of the gas, Trevor Lowe felt little the worse on the following morning for his submersion in the river. This was due entirely to White's drastic measures, for as soon as he had succeeded in bringing the dramatist back to consciousness, he had hurried him with all speed to Monk's Lodge; and, with the assistance of Shadgold and the others, who were hastily awakened, Lowe had been put to bed with a large dose of hot whisky.

The inquest on Ogden had been fixed for that morning, and after a hasty breakfast the four of them set out for Friar's Vale, leaving White in charge of the cottage. They reached the school-room where the inquiry was being held with a minute to spare.

The entire population of Friar's Vale,

with a fair number of people from Dryseley, seemed to have turned up for the occasion, for the small room was packed; but if these spectators had come in the hope of hearing any sensational developments, they were disappointed, as the proceedings were of the briefest.

The coroner took Dr. McGuire's evidence regarding the cause of death, and Trevor Lowe gave an account of how the discovery of the body had been made. This was confirmed by ack and Tony. Then Inspector Jesson, acting on Shadgold's instructions, applied for and was granted a fortnight's adjournment.

Mr. Wyse, who had been present at the proceedings, tried to buttonhole Lowe as he left the building; but the playwright, who was anxious to get away, hurriedly excused himself. Leaving the grey-haired man chatting to Tony and Jack, he took Shadgold to one side.

'I'm going over to Dryseley,' he said. 'There are one or two inquiries that I want to make over there. I don't suppose I shall be very long.'

'Do you want me to come with you?'

Lowe shook his head. 'No, it isn't necessary.'

'Well, be careful,' said Shadgold. 'Don't forget, there have already been two attempts made on your life. These people, whoever they are, aren't likely to stop at that. The third may be more successful.'

'They rather took me by surprise last night,' replied the dramatist. 'I must admit that I wasn't prepared for the gas arrangement, but they won't do it again. I shall be on guard in future.' He left Shadgold with a nod of farewell, and set off towards Dryseley.

The offices of the late Mr. William P. Ogden, which were his objective, were situated in the narrow High Street. Upon entering, Lowe handed his card to the office-boy who came to inquire his business.

'I should like to see whoever is in charge,' he said.

'You mean Mr. Wishart, sir?' asked the boy brightly, and Lowe nodded. The boy disappeared into an inner room, and after a few seconds' delay returned.

'Will you come this way, sir, please,' he said, and Lowe was ushered into a shabby but comfortably furnished room and greeted by a smile from the youngish-looking man who was sitting behind a broad littered desk.

'What can I do for you, Mr. Lowe?' he said, rising and holding out his hand.

'I want to ask you a few questions, Mr. Wishart,' said the dramatist, gripping the extended hand. 'I'm looking into this matter of Mr. Ogden's death on behalf of my friend, Inspector Shadgold. I presume you're carrying on the business?'

The other nodded and waved him to a chair. 'Yes,' he said as Lowe sat down. 'I was his chief clerk, and I'm looking after things until the solicitors have wound up the estate. It's a terrible business, isn't it? The murder, I mean. Why anybody wanted to kill Ogden is beyond me. He was a most popular man, and as far as I know, hadn't an enemy in the world. What happened at the inquest? I was expecting a subpoena, and was rather surprised that I didn't get one.'

He pushed a box of cigarettes across the desk, and Lowe took one. 'The whole inquiry was adjourned for a fortnight,' said the dramatist. 'There isn't sufficient evidence at present to put before the coroner that would enable him to bring in a satisfactory verdict. The adjournment will give the police time to make further investigations. Now, Mr. Wishart, I've come to see you because I presume that you're almost as well acquainted with the business as Mr. Ogden himself.'

'You mean this estate business?' said the young man. 'Yes, I think I can say that I am. As a matter of fact, I don't mind telling you — in confidence, of course — that I have already applied to the solicitors for permission to make an offer to buy the goodwill and run the business myself.'

'Excellent! Then you'll be able to supply me with the information I require. You were, I believe, responsible for the letting of Monk's Lodge?'

Mr. Wishart nodded and leaned back in his chair. 'That is so,' he said.

'The place, I understand,' Lowe continued, 'belongs to a certain Mr. and Mrs. Cheply, who are at present on holiday in America?'

'Perfectly correct,' said Mr. Wishart. 'To

be exact, they are in Philadelphia.'

'How long has Monk's Lodge belonged to them?'

'Some years, I believe,' answered the younger man. 'I can't be quite sure of that because it was before my time. I've only been with this business for a little over three years.'

'You don't know, then, whether anybody else owned the property prior to it coming into the Cheplys' possession?'

Mr. Wishart shook his head. 'No,' he replied; 'it's been theirs as long as I can remember.'

'Have you got a copy of the title-deeds or the lease, or whatever it is that proves their possession of the place?' asked Lowe.

Again Mr. Wishart shook his head. 'I'm afraid not. They're in the hands of the Cheplys' solicitors.'

'Would it be possible to see them?'

'If you could get Mr. Cheply's authorisation, there should be no difficulty. I doubt very much if they would let you see them without that. They're a rather old-fashioned firm. I'm not speaking without a certain amount of reason,' he went on. 'Mr. Ogden wanted to see them himself some time ago in connection with a clause regarding some repairs. The solicitors refused without the authority of Mr. Cheply, but as they were able to supply Mr. Ogden with the information he wanted, we didn't bother to get the necessary permission.'

'I see.' Lowe considered for a moment. 'I suppose you have Mr. Cheply's address in Philadelphia?' he asked.

The other replied in the affirmative.

'Then I should be very glad,' went on the dramatist, 'if you would cable them asking them to instruct their solicitors to let you have all the documents relating to their ownership of Monk's Lodge. I will, of course, pay any expenses that may be incurred.'

The young man hesitated. 'Can you give me your reasons for wishing to see these documents?' he asked.

'I could,' Lowe replied candidly; 'but if you'll excuse me I'd rather not at the moment. I don't mind telling you this much, however: it is merely to destroy or substantiate a rather vague theory that I've got at the back of my mind.'

'Connected with Mr. Ogden's death?'

inquired Wishart.

'Very closely connected if I'm right,' answered Lowe.

Stretching out his hand, Wishart pressed a bell on his desk. 'All right; I'll send the cable,' he said, and Lowe thanked him.

The bright-faced office-boy appeared in answer to the summons, and Mr. Wishart asked him to bring the Cheplys' address. While the lad went to search for it, he drew a sheet of paper towards him and wrote rapidly, pushing it across to the dramatist when he had finished. 'Is that what you want?' he asked.

Lowe read the brief message and nodded. 'That'll do admirably, Mr. Wishart,' he replied. 'It's exceedingly kind of you. I'm passing the post office on my way back, so I'll dispatch this myself in order to save time.'

The boy returned with a filing-card. Adding the address to the draft of the cable, Lowe rose to take his leave.

'I hope you'll let me know if this leads to anything,' said Wishart as they shook hands. 'Naturally I shall be interested to hear of any discovery that will throw a light on poor

Ogden's tragic death.'

Lowe promised and left the offices.

The post office was at the end of the High Street and was empty when Lowe handed in the cable, but as he was gathering up his change the swing-door was pushed open and a man came in hurriedly. He stopped dead as he saw the dramatist, and his face went white. At that moment Lowe looked up and caught sight of the stranger. For a fleeting second he merely thought the man had suddenly been taken ill, and then something oddly familiar about the face struck him. It was the man who had driven the car the day he had arrived at King's Hayling Station!

11

The House in York Road

For the tenth part of a second, the man stared at Trevor Lowe as though he had seen a ghost. Then, swinging round on his heel, he bolted for the exit and disappeared through the swing doors into the street.

When Lowe reached the steps of the post office, he was walking rapidly on the other side of the road, glancing back quickly every now and again over his shoulder. The dramatist's brain worked swiftly. He wanted to find out who the man was and where he lived. As far as he could see, there were only two alternatives by which this result could be achieved, and neither appealed to him.

The first was to follow the man and have him arrested, in which case it was very doubtful whether he would learn anything, since he had no proof to offer the police that would warrant them detaining him.

The second was to shadow the man himself and find out where he went — which was equally futile, for it could not be carried out without his quarry becoming aware of the fact. And then, as he watched the receding figure hurrying away down the street, a third suggestion offered itself in the shape of a rather ragged youth who was approaching, carrying a parcel. Lowe beckoned him into the shadow of the post-office doorway.

'Wotcher want?' asked the lad doubtfully.

'Listen,' said Lowe quickly. 'Here's half-a-crown. I want you to follow that man hurrying down the street there — the one in the brown overcoat and cap. Don't let him know you're following him, but find out where he goes and then come back and report to me here. I'll give you ten shillings for your trouble.'

The ragged youth's eyes opened wide. ''Alf a quid!' he exclaimed incredulously. 'Do yer mean it, guv'nor?'

'Of course I do!' rapped Lowe swiftly. 'Now hurry, or you'll miss him.'

'All right, I'm on!' said the lad. He pocketed his half-crown and, without waiting for a second bidding, was off in the wake of the man with the brown coat.

From the cover of the post-office doorway Lowe watched them both disappear round a side turning, and then considered what he should do next. Until the boy returned, he could not leave the vicinity of the post office, otherwise he might miss him. And how long the lad was likely to be was impossible to conjecture. It rested entirely on where the man in the brown coat was going. The look of shocked surprise when he had come face to face with the dramatist in the post office had convinced Lowe that he knew all about the attempt of the previous night to drown him in the River Loam. The man had looked as though he had seen a ghost, and for a brief moment he probably considered that he had! Without knowing that the dramatist had been rescued, it must have been a shattering surprise to suddenly come upon the man he believed to be at the bottom of the river, alive and well and in the flesh.

A thing that puzzled Lowe and occupied a good deal of his thoughts while he waited for the return of the boy was that he was certain he had seen the man somewhere before, apart from the time he had driven the car from King's Hayling to Monk's Lodge. His face struck a chord of memory, and although it set it vibrating, no coherent picture resulted. Somewhere and at some time Lowe had run across the man and he racked his brains vainly to try to recollect where it was and under what circumstances. It was like searching for a word that for a moment eluded him — he knew it perfectly, but for the life of him could not grasp it. Sooner or later it would come to him. It was useless trying to force his memory to work.

Crossing over to a little paper shop on the opposite side of the road, he bought a local paper and returned to his position on the post-office steps. He had read nearly the entire contents of the paper before the ragged youth put in an appearance.

'I've found out where he went all right, guv'nor,' he said, with a look of relief at finding the dramatist still there. 'He went into a house at the end of a lot of new ones they're building in York Road — Number 31 it was.'

Lowe took a ten-shilling note from his

pocket and placed it in the boy's eager palm. 'You've done very well, my lad,' he said. 'How far is York Road from here?'

'About two mile, I should think, sir,' the boy answered, after a lengthy calculation. 'It's right outside the town — almost in the country. Yer can't mistake it, though, 'cause the road's up and there's piles of bricks and slates and things where they're building.'

'All right; I'll be able to find it from that,' said Lowe with a nod of dismissal, and the ragged youth scampered away clutching his newly acquired wealth.

Lowe folded his paper, put it in his pocket, and walked slowly along the High Street in the opposite direction. He had, at any rate, learnt the destination of the man in the brown coat, but he decided to wait until darkness had fallen before making any personal investigation of the place. Should No. 31 York Road prove to be the head-quarters of the men who had twice made an attempt on his life, and who were in some way bound up with the mystery surrounding Monk's Lodge, he did not want to scare them away by allowing himself to be seen in the neighbourhood of their retreat in daylight. Darkness would offer a friendly cloak to conceal his movements.

The question now was how to while away the time until it was sufficiently dark for his purpose. It was a long way from Dryseley to Monk's Lodge, and Lowe felt no very great inclination to do the double journey twice, for the only means of getting there and back again was to walk. It was true he could have used the car on the return journey, but then he would have to find somewhere to leave it, and a far simpler method was to remain in Dryseley until he had completed what he proposed to do. A slight feeling of hunger suggested to him how a portion of the time at least could be put to good use.

On the outskirts of the town he found an unpretentious but very comfortable-looking inn, and succeeded in obtaining an excellent meal of cold beef, homemade pickles, bread and cheese, and a pint of beer. By the time he had finished this repast it was nearly three o'clock, and he spent the rest of the afternoon in the bar-parlour chatting to the host, a genial man who was filled with a stream of local gossip concerning Friar's Vale, Dryseley and King's Hayling, which he was not averse to pouring forth on the slightest encouragement.

During that afternoon Lowe acquired a considerable amount of out-of-the-way knowledge regarding the locality and certain of the inhabitants. About Monk's Lodge the landlord was voluble. There was something queer about the place, and he said there always had been. He had not been at all surprised to hear that a murder had been committed there; in fact, it was just the sort of thing he would have expected in a place like that. Look where it was built: on the site of an old monastery, the ruins of which could still be seen. No wonder the place was haunted. No, he had not seen anything himself, but he had heard stories, and he knew several people who had seen the ghostly monk that was supposed to wander about the place. About four or five years ago Monk's Lodge had been a favourite spot for the courting couples of the district, but one or two scares and tales of the things they had seen soon made it unpopular.

Lowe listened to this and a lot more like it. Apparently the ghostly gentleman who wandered about in a monk's robe had got tired of his nocturnal rambles, or had been engaged elsewhere for a long period, for he learned that nothing had been seen or heard of him from the time of the first scare until just recently — in fact, just before Jack and Tony had arrived at the cottage.

He stayed at the inn for tea and was served with an epicurean repast of hot scones, homemade jam, and a large dish of cream. By the time he had eaten a portion of this and smoked several pipes thoughtfully — for the landlord's conversation had supplied him with several things that were worth thinking about — dusk was beginning to fall, and he concluded that it was time to set off on his voyage of discovery to York Road.

York Road, he found after an hour's brisk walk, was merely the embryo of a road. In other words, it was a road that was in the process of construction. The beginning of it consisted of a long row of uniform villas with neatly tended patches of front garden, their brick and paint work so new that it was obvious they had only recently been built. A short distance on, however, these houses ceased abruptly, though the presence at odd intervals of scaffolding and piles of red bricks and slates tended to show that in the near future this orderly array of desirable residences would be extended.

Among none of these did Lowe find the house he was seeking, and it was not until he had passed a blank open space and come to a row of much older houses that he found it. These houses were larger and infinitely gloomier, and had apparently been in existence for some years. Lowe watched the numbers as he walked in a leisurely fashion on the opposite side of the road. 26, 29, 30, 31—that was it! Passing slowly, Lowe glanced over covertly at the building. There were no lights, and the windows were curtainless.

'Odd,' he muttered as he stopped in the shadow of a clump of trees. 'The place looks deserted. Could that fellow have discovered that the boy was following him and led him here as a blind?'

He stood pondering for a moment before he made up his mind, and then walking further along, he crossed the road and came back on the other side. At the dilapidated gate of No. 31 he slowed, and, with a quick glance up and down the road, slipped into the weed-choked front garden.

There were three worn stone steps leading up to the front door, which had once been painted green but was now a nondescript colour that blended with the dust and grime that covered the frosted glass panels on either side. Standing on the threshold, Lowe took stock of the lower front part of the house. There was a basement window not visible from the pavement owing to the high growth of the straggling hedge, and behind this window the dramatist caught a glimpse of dirty white shutters, one of which was half off its hinges and hanging at a drunken angle. He examined the front door closely and saw that the keyhole could not have been used for at least several weeks, for an enterprising spider had built a web across it that was unbroken.

He frowned. The wild goose chase theory seemed to have been borne out. The man had evidently guessed that he was being trailed and had led the boy to this empty house in order to throw him off the scent.

And then, just as he had reached this

conclusion, Lowe discovered something that made him alter his mind.

Happening to glance down, he saw in the half-light that preceded the approaching night a clear track of footprints in the soft mould. There was not merely one trail, but many, and they all led to the basement window with the broken shutter.

The dramatist left the front doorsteps and dropped cautiously into the well of the basement. Pressing his hand against the protruding framework of the lower half of the window, he pressed gently upwards. The window slid up noiselessly, and a touch of his fingers in the grooves told him that they had been carefully oiled. Hoisting himself gingerly over the sill, he stepped into the darkness beyond and carefully closed the window behind him. Standing motionless for a second, he listened intently, but no sound reached his ears; and, after a momentary hesitation, he took his torch from his pocket and pressed the button.

As he had half expected, he was standing in an empty kitchen. There was no furniture of any kind, but the trail of footprints was still plainly visible in the thick dust that coated the floor. They led to a door at the far end, and Lowe made his way over to it. Pushing it open, he found on the other side a flight of narrow stairs leading upwards. Ascending these, but keeping to the sides to avoid them creaking, he came to another door, which he found opened into the hall and faced the front entrance. This area, like the kitchen, was bare and unfurnished, and a glance into the two rooms that occupied either side of it showed him that they, too, were empty and uninhabited.

He decided to see what lay in the upper part of this gloomy and silent house and went on up the stairs. On the first floor there was nothing beyond accumulated dust and two broken chairs that had evidently been left behind by the previous tenants. There was now only one more floor to explore, and Lowe made his way cautiously up the last flight of stairs. There were two doors on this narrow landing, one on the right and one on the left, and Lowe chose the one on the right.

Turning the handle, he pushed it softly open and then paused with a stifled exclamation, for this room was furnished and there was distinct evidence that it had been recently occupied. In the centre was a plain deal table and three chairs, and on the table stood a couple of glasses that had been used during the past few hours, for they still contained the dregs of drink. There was no carpet on the floor, but the window on the far side had been carefully screened by having several old sacks nailed across it.

Lowe stepped across the threshold, his right hand clenched, every nerve alert. One step forward he took, and then a slight sound behind him made him swing round. But he was too late! He caught a momentary glimpse of two dark eyes set in a white face and a little wisp of black beard, and then something descended on his head and the picture split into an irregular eruption of orange flame and — darkness!

12

The Death Chamber

When Trevor Lowe recovered consciousness, he found that he had been securely bound in one of the chairs. The candle
had been lighted and the room was now
occupied by two men. He could see little
of their faces, for they had taken the precaution of covering the lower halves, from
the eyes downwards, with handkerchiefs
knotted behind their heads. There was a
throbbing pain in his head, and his right
arm and shoulder ached from his fall.

As he opened his eyes, one of the men
came over and stood looking down at him.
'So you've recovered, have you?' he grunted.
'I thought I'd finished you at first.'

'I'm not so easily finished,' retorted
the dramatist. 'And for your own good, I
suggest that you put an end to this nonsense
and release me at once.'

The other chuckled softly. 'Anything

to oblige you, Mr. Lowe,' he sneered. 'Anything in fact, but that! You see, you've been a great source of trouble to us, and I personally dislike trouble very much indeed.'

'You appear to spend most of your time looking for it,' said Lowe, 'and this business is going to land you into a lot of trouble, unless I'm very much mistaken.'

'I think for once *you* are mistaken,' replied his captor, 'and certainly if there's any trouble coming it won't emanate from you! After tonight you won't be in a position to trouble anybody!'

'That sounds an alarming threat, Murdock,' said Lowe, looking up at the man steadily.

He started. 'So you know me, do you?' he said, almost in a whisper.

'I recognised you just before you struck that blow,' he answered curtly, 'in spite of the fact that you've tried to disguise yourself by growing a beard. The last time I saw you, you were in the dock at the Old Bailey.'

'Yes, and it was you who put me there,' snarled the man savagely. 'If you'd only stick to your own job and not start poking your nose into things that don't concern you, you'd be better off. I always swore I'd get even with you for putting Shadgold on my track. Now it's my turn.'

'Your turn won't come, Murdock,' said the dramatist, 'until they wake you at eight and make you dress in your own clothes with the exception of your collar and take you for that little walk that leads from the condemned cell to the death-house.'

The man before him uttered an exclamation. 'Hold your tongue!' he snapped, and leaning forward, struck Lowe deliberately across the mouth. His knuckles cut the dramatist's lip, and a thin trickle of blood ran slowly over his chin.

'That's the sort of action I would have expected from you, Murdock,' he said in a level voice, though his eyes flashed dangerously.

'I wish that bullet had got you in the car,' hissed Murdock furiously.

'Or that I'd drowned the other night as you intended,' cut in Lowe quickly.

The other man, who up to now had remained silent, came forward. 'What's the good of all this talking?' he growled. 'Let's finish the business and get away.'

Murdock choked down his rage with an effort. 'You're right,' he said. 'We're wasting time.'

'I entirely agree with you,' murmured Lowe. 'May I ask what exactly you intend to do?'

'I should have thought,' sneered Murdock, 'that your powers of deduction would have already told you. Perhaps if you take a look at the fireplace and the door you'll be able to guess.'

Lowe followed the direction of his gaze and saw what he had missed seeing before: that the fireplace had a sheet of brown paper carefully pasted over it. Shifting his eyes to the door, he saw that a beading of felt had been nailed round the edge.

'The window has also been attended to,' went on Murdock as he watched the dramatist, and saw by his expression that he had taken in the meaning of these preparations. 'When the door is shut, it's impossible for any air whatsoever to get into this room — it's also impossible for anything else to get out!' He paused and pointed to the wall directly facing Lowe. 'That gas jet is convenient, and before we go I intend to turn it on. I don't think there's any need to say more — the rest can safely be left to your imagination.'

'You appear to be rather fond of gas!' said the dramatist coolly. 'I might say in more sense than one.'

'It can be put to many excellent uses,' retorted Murdock, ignoring Lowe's last words, 'and I can think of no better one than this. It is a slow death, and you'll have plenty of time to prepare for the end. I've been considerate enough to choose it for that reason.'

'And you imagine that you can get away with it!' asked Lowe, his mind working quickly to try to find some way of getting out of this death-trap.

'I do!' replied the other. 'Nobody knows you're here — you've had no opportunity to tell anyone. Had you done so, this scheme would never have been put into operation. You see, we were a little too clever for you,' he went on. 'My friend —' He nodded in the direction of the other man, who was standing by the table impatiently drumming on the top with his fingers. '—was perfectly aware that he was being followed this morning. I was in this house when he arrived, and returned the compliment by following your messenger, and afterwards you yourself! I guessed that sooner or later you'd be paying a visit to this house, and arranged my plans accordingly. You see, it was quite simple.'

'I don't know what you want to waste all this time for,' broke in his companion irritably. 'For God's sake, let's do what we're going to do and get away from here!'

'Don't be impatient,' said Murdock. 'We're going now; only, I shouldn't have liked to leave Mr. Lowe without plenty to think about! There will be quite an interval between the time I turn on the gas and the time the fumes overcome him!'

He took a handkerchief from his pocket and bound it tightly over the dramatist's mouth. 'It's unlikely that anyone would hear you even if you shouted,' he said pleasantly, 'for in rendering this room air-tight we've practically made it sound-proof, but still it's just as well to take precautions. It would be a pity if the plan was spoiled through overlooking a small detail.' He stopped and looked quickly round the room. 'You can blow out the candle now,' he said to his companion.

The other man obeyed, and in the darkness that followed Lowe heard him walk across the bare floor, and then the hiss of the gas as the tap was turned on fully. A slight draught reached him as the door opened and the two men passed out.

Just before it was closed again, Murdock called a mocking farewell. 'Goodbye, Mr. Lowe, and sleep well!'

The dramatist heard the key grate in the lock and the sound of retreating footsteps. They died away in the distance, leaving a deathly silence that was broken only by the insistent hissing from the gas jet.

The moment the door was closed, Lowe set to work to try to loosen the cords that bound him to the chair, but his wrists had been bound separately behind his back and pulled so tightly that they had cut into his flesh. No amount of effort on his part succeeded in shifting them a fraction of an inch.

After ten minutes of tugging and straining he paused, panting from his exertion, and then he became aware that already the air was heavy and unbreathable. The blood was pounding like fury in the veins of his neck, a heavy pressure like a band of iron constricted his forehead, and his lungs ached as they fought for more oxygen. A dreamy lassitude overtook him, and he felt an almost overpowering desire to close his eyes and let his senses slip away. Exercising all his willpower, he succeeded in overcoming this fatal sleepiness, for he knew that once he allowed himself to give way, the transition from unconsciousness to death would be imperceptible. With redoubled energy, he strove to free himself from his bonds.

In the midst of his frantic struggles, one of the back legs of the chair broke and it toppled over backwards, carrying the dramatist with it. His head struck the lower part of the wall and, with a faint groan, consciousness left him for the second time. He lay huddled up and motionless while the air became more and more laden with the fumes of death!

13

The Second Warning

Tony Frost's hand hovered over the chessboard. With an expression of the utmost concentration, he removed one of White's bishops with the only remaining knight that was left to him.

'That's quite a good move,' said White with a grin, and he pushed his queen forward two paces.

'Here, where are you going?' demanded Tony as he rose to his feet.

'I'm going to finish my book.'

'Aren't you going on with the game?' asked Tony in surprise.

'There's no game to go on with,' said White with a laugh. 'I've got your king in the corner and you can't get out of it.'

'By Jove, you know,' Tony said after a few moments' consideration, 'I really believe you *have* done it!'

'Got it in the neck, Tony?' asked Jack,

looking up from his book and winking at White.

'Absolutely,' said Tony with a sigh, and getting up from the table he went over to the sideboard. 'I think I shall drown my sorrows in drink after that!' he remarked. 'What about you, White?'

Lowe's secretary nodded. 'Thanks,' he said.

'You'll have one too, won't you, Jack? And you, sir?' He looked across at Inspector Shadgold, who with wrinkled brows was immersed in a crossword puzzle.

'Thank you, just a small one, and not too much soda,' said the burly inspector.

'Same for me,' broke in Jack.

Tony poured out the drinks and White squirted in the soda. They carried the glasses over to the other two, and Tony was in the act of raising his when an exclamation from White made him pause with the glass halfway to his lips. 'What's the matter?' he asked.

White was standing by the chessboard, his eyes fixed on the pieces which had not been disturbed. 'Look!' he whispered excitedly, and pointed.

Tony came over to his side and glanced down in the direction of his finger. In the centre of the chessboard, firmly embedded in the wood and still quivering, was a slender knife! Round the hilt a piece of paper had been wrapped and secured with thread.

'Good God!' exclaimed Inspector Shadgold, who had joined the group and was staring over White's shoulder. 'How did that get there?'

'Through the window,' snapped White. 'I heard it strike the board a second ago!' With a quick movement he removed the paper from the handle and unfolded it. Roughly printed in irregular capitals were the words:

* * *

'YOU HAVE BEEN WARNED ONCE. THIS WILL BE THE LAST WARNING. GO!'

Without a word, he handed the message to the others, and flashed a quick look at the open window. Whoever had thrown the knife, he thought, could not be very far away at that very moment. Wheeling round, he made for the door.

'Where are you going?' asked Shadgold, looking round quickly.

'To see if I can find the fellow who threw that knife,' snapped White.

'I'll come with you,' growled the Scotland Yard man, and he followed him out into the hall while Jack and Tony crowded at his heels.

Outside, the dusky shadows of twilight made it impossible to see very clearly beyond the straggling hedgerow at the far end of the lawn; but White, who was several yards ahead of the others, thought he saw a dark figure disappearing through a gap in the hedge. He broke into a run and arrived at the place in time to catch a second glimpse of the fugitive form as it dived into the maze of trees beyond.

White vaulted the hedge and, without pausing a second, bounded forward in pursuit. He heard the heavy footfalls of Shadgold behind him, but he could see nothing of his quarry. Then suddenly there came a shout from Tony. 'There he goes!' he cried excitedly. 'To the left there!'

White altered his direction and a moment later caught a glimpse of a gaunt figure flitting through the trees about forty yards ahead. Even in the dim light of the dying day it was possible to distinguish the long robe and cowl. 'It's the monk!' breathed White. 'After him!'

Jack and Tony had outpaced the heavier-footed inspector and drawn level with White. 'That's the same fellow I saw the other night,' panted the former.

'With a bit of luck we'll get him this time,' gasped White, and he put on a spurt.

But the figure ahead had disappeared behind a clump of bushes, and when they reached the spot there was no sign of it. They strained their eyes, peering into the gloom in front on either side, but the monk had completely vanished!

'Confound it!' grated White with annoyance. 'We've lost him!'

They searched around among the tangled undergrowth and scattered patches of bushes, all four taking a different direction, but without result.

'It's no good going on now,' said White disappointedly when they met again at the place where their quarry had eluded them. 'I don't know where the fellow went to, but he's gone, and it's useless searching any more in this light. We had better get back.'

'It's uncanny the way that chap disappeared,' muttered Tony in a slightly awed voice as they retraced their steps towards the cottage.

'I don't know about being uncanny, but it's a damned nuisance,' growled Shadgold. 'I'd like to have had a chance of seeing who he was.'

'So would I,' said White. 'But after all, it wasn't difficult for him to give us the slip. He probably knows these woods much better than we do, and he had the added advantage of it being almost dark.'

'I wonder what's at the bottom of all this business,' said Jack after they had gone for a short while in silence.

'That's what I'm going to find out,' said the Scotland Yard man. 'I wonder what's keeping Mr. Lowe?' he added as an afterthought. 'When he left us this morning he said he wouldn't be long, and he's been away all day.'

'Perhaps he's found something,' said White. 'What was he going over to Dryseley for?'

'He didn't say,' replied Shadgold, shaking his head. 'All he said was that he had some inquiries to make. I didn't like to ask him what they were. You know how fond he is of keeping everything to himself until he's got it worked out to his satisfaction.'

White smiled. He did know only too well this peculiarity of the dramatist's, and it had often irritated him almost beyond endurance.

They were crossing the lawn when Jack suddenly grasped White by the arm and stopped dead. 'Look!' he exclaimed. 'There's somebody in the dining-room!'

White looked and saw the figure of a man pass between the lamp and the window. 'It's probably Mr. Lowe come back,' he said, hurrying forward. 'But we'd better make sure.'

But it was not Trevor Lowe, as they presently found when they entered the room. Mr. Wyse was standing and gazing intently at a picture on the wall. He turned as they came in.

'I trust that I've not been guilty of an unpardonable liberty,' said the unsuccessful author of crime stories, 'but finding the door open, I naturally expected there'd be someone at home. I called several times, and receiving no answer, I decided to wait.'

'There's no need to apologise at all,' said Jack. 'How's your daughter?'

'She's quite well, thank you,' replied Mr. Wyse. 'She's gone to bed early tonight. The air here makes her feel tired. Where's Mr. Lowe?'

'He hasn't come back yet,' said White.

Mr. Wyse looked interested. 'Is he on the trail?' he asked. 'Has he discovered anything?'

'We don't know what he's doing until he comes home and tells us,' grunted Shadgold. The Scotland Yard man did not like Mr. Wyse, and took very few pains to conceal the fact.

'Hasn't he been back since he left us this morning?' said Wyse almost incredulously, and when White shook his head: 'Dear me — dear me! Something very urgent must have happened to detain him. I'm afraid —' He looked apologetically from one to the other. '—that you will think me very inquisitive, but I take a great interest in crime, or anything appertaining to crime, and this case in particular intrigues me enormously.'

'Perhaps you'd care to stay and have some supper,' said Jack, 'then perhaps you'll have the chance to see Mr. Lowe yourself.'

Mr. Wyse accepted the invitation graciously, and Shadgold turned a ferocious glare on Jack that was entirely wasted, for it is doubtful if that young man ever saw it. Mr. Wyse might be a bore — Jack was quite prepared to admit privately that he was — but he was also the father of a certain extremely attractive woman, and was therefore entitled to a certain amount of respect.

They sat down to a meal of tinned lobster and fresh salad prepared by Tony, who had tacitly constituted himself the chef of the establishment; and although the conversation drifted from one subject to another, White became conscious that Mr. Wyse was doing his best to pump them. Again and again he skilfully led back to the peculiar happenings around Monk's Lodge; and when Jack, in a burst of confidence — for which both Shadgold and White could have cheerfully kicked him — told the guest about the warning on the handle of the knife that had been thrown through the window, Mr. Wyse shook his silver head gravely.

'It's no — er — business of mine,' he said, 'but I can't help feeling that you're all rather foolish in remaining here after what's happened.'

'You surely don't expect us to clear out because of a few threats and a — a lunatic who goes about pretending he's a spook monk?' exclaimed White indignantly.

'I was only suggesting,' said Mr. Wyse hurriedly, 'that it seems positively dangerous to remain and risk your lives for the sake of being stubborn.'

White made no reply, and presently, during a lull in the ensuing conversation, Mr. Wyse looked across at him with rather a thoughtful expression. 'What made you say just now that the monk gentleman is a lunatic?' he asked quietly.

The moment he made that remark, White realised that he had committed a blunder. Only three people knew of the information regarding Joseph Luckman that had come though from the fingerprint department at Scotland Yard: Trevor Lowe, Shadgold, and himself. Lowe had been very emphatic in his wishes that the knowledge should be kept among themselves. Not even Jack and Tony had been informed of the contents of that report.

'Why do I think that he's a lunatic?' he repeated, shrugging his shoulders casually. 'Because it seems the most natural conclusion to draw from his behaviour. Would anyone who was in his right senses spend his time dashing about the country dressed up as a monk?'

The elderly author appeared to regard this explanation as entirely satisfactory. 'I see your point,' he said, nodding. 'Yes, most probably you're right.'

They finished the meal without any sign of Lowe's return. When after a drink and a smoke Mr. Wyse took his departure, Shadgold turned to White rather anxiously. 'Hope nothing's happened to Mr. Lowe,' he said. 'It seems rather extraordinary that he should be away all this time.'

'I've been thinking the same,' said White with a worried frown. 'But I don't see what we can do.'

'We can't do anything,' said Shadgold,

'except wait. But I must admit that I'm getting uneasy. We mustn't forget that there have already been two attempts on his life.'

He was wrong, but he did not know it then. A third attempt had already been made on Lowe's life — and unless a miracle happened, it looked like being successful.

14

No. 31

Trevor Lowe opened his eyes and made a feeble effort to move, but without success. And then, through a jumbled mass of thoughts, he remembered. He was surrounded by impenetrable darkness, and the air was acrid with the smell of gas. The amazing thing was that he was not dead. That he must have been pretty nearly so, he had not the slightest doubt, for his head felt heavy, and he was conscious of a feeling of nausea.

He was still lying on his side on the floor, trussed to the chair that he dimly recalled toppling over after his frantic attempt to loosen his bonds. He had not the slightest idea how long he had remained in this position. It seemed but a few minutes since he had fallen and stunned himself against the wall; but for all he knew it might have been hours, except that in that case surely the gas would have done its work. It was incredible that the poisonous fumes had allowed him to regain consciousness at all.

A peculiar difference in the room gradually forced itself upon his senses. For some little time he puzzled as to what this difference was, and then it came to him. Holding his breath, he strained his ears to catch the sound of that monotonous hissing.

It had ceased!

So that was why he was still alive. Not only had the gas stopped flooding the room, but it must have stopped a long time ago, for no one knew better than he how speedily death came from inhaling even a small amount of carbon monoxide. Why the gas had suddenly stopped, he could not conjecture. But stop it certainly had, and in the nick of time too.

In striking the wall, the gag had become loosened, and by working his jaws Lowe was able to get rid of it altogether. Tautening his muscles, he tried once more to shift the cords that bound him. But he made no impression and presently ceased his efforts, breathing hard, with perspiration running down his forehead.

He lay panting and staring into the darkness. Even though he had escaped death from one source, his position was still far from enviable. He was helpless, in a practically airtight room, the atmosphere of which was already so charged with poisonous fumes that it was almost unbreathable; in a house that had been empty a considerable time and was likely to remain empty for perhaps even a longer period. No one, with the exception of the two men who had planned his death, knew that he was there. Even the ragged youth who had followed the man in the brown coat did not know his name, and although there would probably be a hue and cry when he was missed, it was a hundred-to-one chance that the boy would connect him with the stranger who had given him the ten-shilling note.

Looking at it from all sides, it appeared that he was in an even worse position than he had been before, for now he was faced with the possibility of dying by slow starvation!

The room was at the top of the house, and it was unlikely, even if he shouted, that his voice would be heard by anyone outside.

He tried, but his voice was dry, and all he could produce at first was a hoarse croak. After a little while, however, he was able to make a better effort, and shouted until his throat ached.

Pausing for a moment to recover his breath, Lowe saw the square that was the window merging into a faint grey patch of light behind the sackcloth covering. It was morning!

★　★　★

Just after seven o'clock, a party of workmen came down York Road and began digging operations almost opposite No. 31. At eight-thirty one of the workmen, an enormous labourer weighing about thirteen stone, put down his pick and, wiping his forehead with the back of his hand, produced from the pocket of his coat, which was lying across a heap of debris, half a dozen thick sandwiches and a much-dented thermos flask. Pouring out a cup of steaming hot tea, he gulped down a copious draught of the almost boiling liquid.

'Ah, that's better,' he rumbled with deep

satisfaction. 'What 'ave you got this morning, mate?'

His companion, who was sitting on the stone coping of the low wall that divided the front garden from No. 31 from the pavement, shook his head gloomily. ''Am, *again*!' he replied. ''Am enough to turn you into a bloomin' pig! I'm sick if it!'

'Why don't yer tell the missus that?' said Bert, resuming his breakfast.

'Tell the missus!' The other laughed scornfully. 'Yer can't tell my missus nothing. The other night —'

But Bert was not listening. With the remains of a sandwich halfway to his open mouth, he was staring up at the forbidding exterior of No. 31. 'Did yer 'ear anything?' he asked.

''Ear what sort of thing?'

'Sounded like as if someone was calling,' answered Bert. 'There yer are; listen now, Joe.'

'I can't 'ear nothing,' remarked Joe, shaking his head. 'Yus, I *can*, though,' he added, and looked blankly about him. 'Where's it coming from?'

'Sounds to me as if it was coming from

the top of that there 'ouse,' said Bert, jerking a half-eaten sandwich towards No. 31.

'But it's empty.'

'Well, you come 'ere where I am and listen for yerself,' grunted Bert.

Joe lounged over. 'Blow me if yer ain't right,' he said after listening for a few seconds. 'Sounds to me as if someone was calling for 'elp.'

'We'd better see what's the matter,' said Bert, taking the precaution to consume the remaining portion of his meal.

Opening the gate, they made their way up the short path and tried the front door. 'Can't git in this way,' said Bert. He took a few paces backwards and gazed up at the front of the house. 'See that little winder at the top?' he said, pointing. 'That's where the shouting's coming from. Look 'ere,' he continued after a moment's intensive thought, 'there's a ladder jest up the road where they're building the noo 'ouses. Best thing we can do is to nip along and git it.'

Joe could not offer any better suggestion than this, so they did so. Propping the ladder against the front of the house, Joe held the lower part while Bert went up. The ladder just reached the window. Tapping on the glass, the labourer shouted: 'Anything up in there?'

'I'm locked in and helpless,' came the faint reply. 'See if you can smash the window.'

Bert's eyes widened in his astonishment. 'Why don't yer open it yerself?' he shouted.

'I can't,' was the answer. 'I'm tied up.'

'Bust me!' muttered Bert. 'All right, guv'nor, I'll see what I can do.'

He tried the window, but it was immovable, and, peering through the glass, he saw that the catch had been turned. There was only one thing to do, and Bert did it. Wrapping his handkerchief round his hand, he rapped sharply on the pane above the catch. At his fourth attempt the glass broke, falling inside the room with a little tinkling crash. The workman put his hand through the jagged hole, pushed back the catch, and after a considerable effort succeeded in raising the lower half of the window.

The gust of gas-laden air that puffed out into his face made him cough, but a second later he had torn down the sacking and scrambled into the room. His face was the picture of astonishment as he saw the bound figure of Lowe, but the dramatist gave him no time just then to ask any questions.

'Cut through these ropes, will you?' he said quickly, and with two slashes from Bert's clasp-knife he was free.

He staggered unsteadily to his feet while the labourer, sniffing hard, looked at him suspiciously. 'What's the game?' he asked. 'Bin tryin' to do away with yerself, 'ave yer?'

'Not exactly,' said Lowe, stretching painfully and rubbing his numbed limbs. 'Someone else thought they'd save me the trouble of doing that!'

'Gawd!' said Bert, open-mouthed. 'Yer don't mean yer was locked in 'ere by somebody else?'

'Well, I could hardly have tied myself up and locked the door on the outside,' answered Lowe dryly. 'Apart from the fact that I'm not sufficiently fond of gas to choose that method of shortening my allotted span!'

He walked over to the gas-jet and examined it. The tap was still turned fully on, and he could find nothing in connection with the fitting itself to account for the sudden cessation of the flow. Coming back to the still-gaping labourer, Lowe took a pound note from his pocket and slipped it into the man's hand.

'I'm greatly indebted to you for what you've done,' he said, 'and I should be still further grateful if you'd keep it to yourself.'

'I don't know as I ought ter do that, guv'nor,' he protested. 'I might git in trouble. This 'ere looks a serious matter to me.'

'It *is* a serious matter,' said the dramatist. 'That's why I'm asking you to keep your mouth shut! My name is Trevor Lowe, and I'm assisting Inspector Shadgold of Scotland Yard in investigating the murder up at Monk's Lodge. I don't want this business to become public property, do you understand?'

The workman's face cleared. 'I've 'eard about 'im and that business,' he said. 'All right, guv'nor, I won't say nothin' to no one, and I'll see Joe don't neither.'

'Good!' said Lowe. 'Now, if you don't mind, I think I'll make use of your ladder and get away from here.'

He hoisted himself over the sill and

descended the swaying structure, to the utter astonishment of Joe. Bert came after him; and when the ladder had been removed, and Lowe had impressed on both of them the necessity of keeping the incident quiet, he returned to the house where he had so nearly lost his life and once more entered it by the basement window.

He was curious to discover why the gas had suddenly stopped, and in a little cupboard under the stairs he found the reason. The meter was of the shilling in the slot variety, a fact that the would-be killers had overlooked. It had never occurred to them that there might not be a continuous supply of gas; but the last person to put a shilling in the meter — probably the previous tenant — had used all but a few cubic feet, enough to last about ten minutes. These had given out almost immediately after Lowe had struck his head against the wall. There was nothing else of interest in Number 31, and, gratefully breathing in great draughts of the fresh morning air, the dramatist set off for Monk's Lodge.

Almost the first thing he saw as he passed through Dryseley was his own car standing outside the police station. Lowe ran up the steps and entered the charge-room. Grouped round the sergeant's desk were Shadgold, White and Inspector Jesson. They swung round as he came in, and White uttered an exclamation of surprise.

'Mr. Lowe!' he gasped. 'Where the dickens have you been? We've been worried to death wondering what had happened to you.'

'You had good cause,' said Lowe. 'I've had rather an exciting time.'

He gave them a brief account of what had occurred, and when he had finished Inspector Shadgold whistled softly.

'By Jove, Mr. Lowe,' he exclaimed, 'it must have been a near thing! I suppose you wouldn't know either of these men again?'

'I'd know one of them,' said the dramatist. 'Lew Murdock.'

'Lew Murdock!' cried Shadgold. 'Are you sure?'

'Positive,' answered Lowe. 'Why?'

'Because Lew Murdock was one of the men who was concerned with Joseph Luckman in the Hatton Garden robbery,' said the Scotland Yard man quietly.

15

Ursula's Warning

Jack Denton walked thoughtfully towards the village. The reason he was going to Friar's Vale lay in his pocket in the form of a long list of comestibles that Tony had prepared for the replenishing of the larder, but that was not occupying his mind at the moment.

Before he had left the cottage, Shadgold, White and Lowe had come in, and Jack had listened in horror to a brief account of the dramatist's adventure that had so nearly ended fatally. Although Lowe himself had made light of it, the recital had filled Jack with uneasiness.

What *was* happening at Friar's Vale, and what was behind all these sinister occurrences? When Tony found that delectable residence, he had let them in for something; and although the series of strange events certainly prevented their holiday from becoming in the slightest degree dull, Jack was not at all sure that he would not have welcomed a little dullness. This living in the constant atmosphere of a shilling shocker was all very well, but a little of it went a very long way. Jack candidly admitted to himself that he preferred his thrills between the covers of a book. The Edgar Wallace touch was a little overpowering when you had, so to speak, to live and eat and sleep with it.

The morning was warm and sunny, and Jack, who had plenty of time on his hands and nothing much to do with it, walked slowly. It was pleasant among the empty lanes with the soft air from the meadows fanning one's face — sweet, fresh-scented air that acted like a tonic. His thoughts switched from crime and sudden chance to a more pleasant subject, and it was not perhaps unnatural that the more pleasant subject should take the form of Ursula Wyse.

He came to the conclusion with rather a shock that he must be dangerously near falling in love with her. This was the only way to account for the extraordinarily upsetting effect the thought of her had on him. It never struck him that she had a certain amount of mystery attached to her and that in this lay the greater part of her attraction. He would not have believed it even if he had, and yet it was probably the truth. Mystery in a woman has attracted men since the world began and will continue to do so until the world ends. It is the greatest weapon in her armoury, and the most effective. Even a plain woman has been known to triumph over a prettier rival by the adroit use of it.

And this mystery that hung about Ursula Wyse was all the more potent in that it was not the ordinary mystery of sex, but a mystery in which sex seemed to be mutely calling for assistance, which although he did not realise it, appealed strongly to Jack's protective instincts. The woman was in some sort of trouble — whether her own or somebody else's, that did not matter — and the age-old instinct, an atavistic remnant of the days when knights risked their lives for a smile from their ladies, was stirring in Jack's subconscious mind.

He reached the village and set about methodically making his purchases, but his thoughts were still full of Ursula Wyse. His last call was at the little general shop, to which he and Tony had paid a visit when they had first arrived at Monk's Lodge.

The old lady behind the counter recognised him at once. 'Good morning, sir.'

'Good morning,' said Jack. 'I want ...' He produced his list and proceeded to give his order.

She collected the things together from various odd corners and put them in a little heap on the counter. 'If yer give me them other parcels, I'll make 'em all inter one fer yer,' she said.

Jack surrendered his collection of packages gratefully.

'Maybe now yer've changed yer mind,' she remarked, looking at him with her head to one side as she began to pile the things together on a sheet of brown paper.

'Er — what about?'

'I warned yer agin' Monk's Lodge, and yer friend called it silly tosh,' said the old woman. 'Maybe yer don't think it so silly now, eh?'

She waited, evidently expecting Jack to make some reply to this question; but since he could think of nothing to say, she waited in vain.

'Up in the attic they found him, didn't they — the dead man?' she said, and answered herself by nodding her head several times. 'Aye, and it's not the last they'll find at Monk's Lodge, mister. It's an evil place, and there are things round it what don't like bein' disturbed by 'uman bein's!'

Jack laughed.

'You can laugh,' said the old woman, stooping and pulling from some hidden receptacle a tangled hank of string. 'Maybe that man H'ogden laughed, too — but 'e ain't laughin' now.'

The smile left Jack's face suddenly. For a moment there flashed before his eyes a vivid picture of the dingy attic lit by the wavering light of the lamp — of Lowe's tense face and Tony's white one, and the horrible, huddled figure on the floor with the spreading crimson stain. He could see again that dreadful head … He felt the colour leave his face and was angry with himself for allowing this stupid old woman to upset him. She was staring at him through her faded eyes, her horny fingers busy with the string.

'It was a very terrible thing to have happened,' he said, 'but you don't expect me to believe that Mr. Ogden was murdered by a ghost?'

'I don't expect you to believe nuthin',' retorted the old woman. 'There's them with eyes and ears what can't see or 'ear. All I says is this — leave Monk's Lodge an' Phantom 'Ollow to the people what they belongs to, an' take yer friends with yer. I'm only an old woman and I ain't educated like some folks, but that's *my* advice, and you'd do well to bide by it.'

'What do you mean by 'the people they belong to'?' asked Jack.

She looked at him quickly. 'It was a religious place once,' she answered in a low voice. 'The monks lived there and died there. Maybe they *still* want to live there.'

Jack felt the hair on the back of his neck stir unpleasantly. Was there, after all, some truth in this old woman's belief? That thing he had seen in the wood ...

He turned sharply as he heard a light footstep behind him — and found himself face to face with Ursula Wyse. The colour flooded back into his face, and he was so surprised that he could only stammer out an almost incoherent good morning.

'Good morning, Mr. Denton,' she returned calmly. 'I want a book of stamps, Mrs. Getch, please.'

The old woman slipped round to the post office compartment of the tiny shop. While she fumbled about for the stamps, Jack looked at Ursula in open admiration. She was dressed in a flimsy summer frock of some soft material and a large shady hat. Jack thought she looked cool, and ... searching for a word, he found that 'fragrant' described her best.

The old woman found the stamp book, passed it over the counter, and took the ten-shilling note that Ursula tendered.

'How's your father, Miss Wyse?' asked Jack as she scooped up her change.

'Quite well, thank you,' she replied, and moved towards the door.

Jack racked his brains to try and think of something to say that would detain her. This was far too good a chance to miss, and if Mrs. Getch would only get a move on and finish packing his parcel, there might be a chance of so far extending this fortunate meeting as to walk part of the way back with her.

'How do you like Friar's Vale now that you've settled down?' he said hastily, one eye on the old woman's slow fingers.

'I think it's a beastly place,' answered Ursulsa; and then, as she saw the surprise that the vehemence of her reply had brought to Jack's face, she added: 'I'm — I'm not fond of the country, but Father likes the quiet.'

Jack's mind flew back to the dismantled cottage and the chloroformed figure of its owner that Tony had described to him with much embellishment, and wondered if Mr. Wyse was finding it quite so quiet as he had expected. The momentary thought suggested a fresh topic of conversation.

'Did you hear any more of the burglars?' he enquired.

Ursula's face whitened, and into her eyes came a fleeting look of fear. 'Nothing,' she answered. 'It was dreadful, wasn't it? Inspector Jesson is making enquiries, but we've heard nothing more yet.'

Jack saw out of the corner of his eye that

Mrs. Getch had completed the parcel, and as Ursula turned once more to the door he stepped to the counter, picked up the parcel, flung down five shillings and was at the lady's side. 'Which way are you going?' he asked.

'I'm going back home,' she replied.

'May I walk as far with you?' he begged, falling into step with her and heedless of Mrs. Getch's frantic calls and signals concerning his change.

'Do,' said Ursula, and together they turned up the narrow street.

Jack felt a pleasant thrill pass through him. Her acceptance of his escort had been so spontaneous that he was sure she had welcomed it. A little silence fell between them, broken at last by Ursula.

'Have there been any more strange happenings at Monk's Lodge?' she asked.

He told her about the warning on the knife and the second attempt on Trevor Lowe's life. She listened gravely and, when he had finished, gave a little shiver.

'Why do you stay?' she said. 'Why don't you cut your holiday and go back to London?'

'You're the second person who's suggested that this morning,' he said.

She looked up quickly. 'Who was the other?' she asked.

Jack related an account of Mrs. Getch's conversation.

'I'm not sure that there isn't something in what she says,' said Ursula. 'And anyway, whether there is or not, it's certain that there's some sort of danger at Phantom Hollow. Why don't you leave the place?'

'I don't know,' replied Jack. 'Partly, I suppose, because I must confess that I'm infernally interested in getting to the bottom of the business, and partly because it smacks too much of running away.'

'How absurd,' she scoffed. 'Besides, it's got nothing to do with you or your friends. It's the business of the police to find out.' She paused for a moment, and then went on rapidly, for they were within a few yards of her gate. 'I wish you'd go away,' she said seriously. 'There's danger — real and tangible danger at Monk's Lodge. Go away while you've still got the chance.' There was a vibrating quality to her voice that told Jack she meant every word.

'It's very nice of you to take such an interest in my welfare,' he said. 'But I assure you that even if I personally wished to go — which I do not, for more reasons than one —' The look he gave her brought a faint tinge of red to her cheeks. '—certainly nothing would induce Lowe to go. He's got his claws into this business, and he won't leave it until he's cleared it up.'

'Perhaps it'll clear *him* up,' she said; and then, with her hand on the gate: 'Well, I've warned you, and if you won't take my advice, I can do no more. Anyway, think over what I've said.'

She said goodbye and, opening the gate, walked up the little path to the cottage door. There she turned and waved, then vanished into the house.

On the way back to Monk's Lodge, Jack *did* think over what she had said, and decided that he would keep it to himself. A sufficient number of people seemed anxious already to get them out of Monk's Lodge without his adding to the number by mentioning Ursula's warning.

16

The Secret Passage

'Things are beginning to shape themselves,' Trevor Lowe remarked. 'I think we can almost say with certainty that Joseph Luckman is at the bottom of this extraordinary business.' He was addressing Inspector Shadgold in the dining room at Monk's Lodge.

'Yes, I think that's pretty obvious,' the inspector replied. 'The fact that this man Murdock is in the district bears out your discovery of the fingerprint. There were three people connected with the Hatton Garden Diamond robbery — Luckman, Murdock, and another man called Blane.' He checked them off on his stubby fingers. 'Blane and Murdock got away and we've never been able to find them. We should never have got Luckman if a 'nose' hadn't given him away and we took him while he was asleep.'

'What was Blane like?' asked Lowe.

'Rather a nondescript-looking fellow,' answered the Scotland Yard man. 'Medium height, rather on the thin side, with a pale, rather washed-out complexion and light blue eyes. He's been convicted several times for burglary. Records have got half a dozen photographs of him.'

'Humph!' said Lowe. 'That description would apply quite well to the man who was with Murdock — the man I saw in the post office.'

'I shouldn't be at all surprised if you're right,' Shadgold agreed. 'But what I can't understand is why they're here.'

'Because Luckman's here,' said the dramatist.

'Yes, but why *is* Luckman here?' demanded Shadgold. 'I can understand all three of them coming to a place like this to lie low. If they wanted to keep out of the way of the police, they couldn't have found a better locality; but if they're at the bottom of the murder of Ogden and all the rest of the things that are taking place — and I'm not doubting that they are — they're going out of their way to draw attention to themselves.'

'They are none of them here because they want to lie low,' declared Lowe emphatically. 'They're here for a very different purpose. I learnt rather an extraordinary piece of information, in a roundabout way, today.' He looked across at White. 'And it concerns our friend the monk, whose appearance last night you were telling me about, Arnold. While I was whiling away the time in Dryseley, I came across an inn with a very loquacious landlord who was full of information regarding the local superstitions that surrounded Monk's Lodge.'

Shadgold sniffed disgustedly. 'It's a mystery to me how people can allow themselves to believe in such nonsense,' he said. 'Surely you're not attaching any importance to that kind of gossip, Mr. Lowe?'

'I am,' answered Lowe, 'because as a direct result of it I am provided with a very curious fact. Apparently this place has always been regarded by the villagers with a certain amount of awe. But so far as I was able to gather yesterday, there was no real foundation for this until four years ago, when various people declared that they had seen a shadowy figure of a monk moving about the woods.'

He paused and the inspector grunted. Lowe continued: 'The curious thing that I want you to note is this — from then until a few days ago, this mysterious phantom monk ceased to appear! When I say ceased to appear, I mean that nobody saw him.'

White looked puzzled. 'I suppose you're driving at something,' he said, 'but I'm hanged if I can see what it is.'

'Well, I'll tell you,' went on his employer, 'and I'm surprised that you haven't seen it for yourselves. If you think for a moment, you'll see that this period of inactivity on the part of the monk corresponds remarkably closely with the period of time spent by Mr. Joseph Luckman in Broadmoor Criminal Lunatic Asylum!'

'By Jove!' exclaimed his secretary excitedly. 'Of course! You mean that Luckman and the monk are one and the same person?'

'That's my theory,' Lowe said.

'But why should Luckman go round masquerading as a monk?' exclaimed Shadgold. 'Why should he write melodramatic warnings on the window of this cottage? Why, above all, should he murder Ogden?'

'Now you're going too fast.' The dramatist smiled. 'I could suggest a reason, but I'd rather not at the moment.'

'The only reason that I can see,' said White, 'is that the man's mad.'

'That would be a very good reason, too,' said Lowe; 'but I don't think that it happens to be the correct one in this case. I'll admit that I don't think Luckman is normal, but I very much doubt if he's insane. With regard to my own idea concerning the motive behind this strange business, I shall be in a better position to speak when I get a reply to certain inquiries I've set on foot.'

'Is that what you went over to Dryseley for?' asked his secretary curiously.

'That was what I went for,' replied the dramatist. 'I'm rather curious,' he went on, rising to his feet, 'to see the place where our friend the monk vanished so suddenly last night.'

'I'll show you,' said White, aware by his employer's sudden changing of the conversation that he did not want to answer any more questions.

'You coming with us, Shadgold?' asked Lowe as he followed White to the door.

Shadgold looked at his watch and shook his head. 'Can't, Mr. Lowe,' he answered. 'I've got to go down to Friar's Vale and see Jesson. See you again at lunch-time.'

Lowe nodded and went out with White. They cut across the garden and, forcing their way through the straggling hedge, passed into the gloom of the wood.

'This is the place,' said White after they had gone about three hundred yards. 'That's where we last saw him — just by that patch of bushes.'

Trevor Lowe looked about him quickly and then began a close examination of the surrounding undergrowth. Parting the thickly growing bushes, he peered into their midst. For nearly half an hour he continued his search, working his way round in a slowly widening circle; and then White, who had become separated from him, heard him give a little exclamation of satisfaction. The dramatist had crawled into the midst of a mass of brambles; and when White, at the expense of a torn coat and severely scratched hands, had succeeded in reaching his side, he saw that Lowe was looking down into a yawning black cavity. The edges were uneven and jagged, and the roots of the dense bushes that surrounded the brink showed like thin white tendrils through the crumbling soil.

'What is it?' asked White, peering over Lowe's shoulder.

'I wouldn't like to say definitely,' answered the dramatist, 'but I certainly think that it's worth looking into — and that's not intended for a pun!'

He took his torch from his pocket and sent a shaft of light stabbing down into the pit. About ten feet below was a jumbled heap of earth, dead leaves and broken branches, while the light revealed on either side two dark, cave-like apertures.

'It looks to me like an underground passage of some sort,' murmured Lowe, 'and it's fairly plain to see what's happened. At some time or other the roof at this point has fallen in, making a midway entrance — an entrance, I should say, that someone has found very convenient, judging from those footprints.' He pointed to the deep indentations on the fallen earth. 'I think

I'll see where this leads to,' he said, and jumped.

He landed in the centre of the earthy mound and looked up. 'Come on!' he called.

White followed him, filled with curiosity.

'We'll try this way first,' said Lowe, nodding towards the right-hand aperture, 'and then work back and explore the other side.'

The route he had chosen proved to be fairly easy going. The floor was made of brick, smooth and regular; and the walls and roof, of the same material, were fairly wide apart and arched a foot above their heads.

'They made a good job of this,' the dramatist remarked. 'I've no doubt that this is a relic of the old monastery.'

White flashed the light ahead, flooding the dark tunnel for fifty yards or more. 'I wonder what the monks used it for,' he said.

'The old-time monks were very cunning people,' replied Lowe, glancing about him with interest, 'and at times not altogether above suspicion in their behaviour.'

The passage ran straight for nearly two

hundred yards and then it veered sharply to the right, dipping slightly, and a little further on they emerged into a large cell-like chamber about twelve feet square. The atmosphere was stale and dank, and the walls, reinforced by large slabs of stone, oozed moisture and were covered by irregular patches of green slime.

'This looks like a dungeon of sorts,' remarked Lowe as White sent the white ray of the torch travelling about the place. 'Look at that!' The dramatist pointed at one of a row of heavy iron rings firmly embedded in the wall, attached to which were uneven lengths of chain half-eaten away with rust. In a tragic heap immediately below one of these rings was a little pile of brownish-white bones, and nearby an oval-shaped object grinned up hideously with toothless jaws.

'I wonder who the poor wretch was,' muttered Lowe, eyeing the decayed skeleton grimly. 'Some unfortunate monk, I suppose, who had offended against the laws of the monastery.'

White gave a little involuntary shiver as something flitted across the floor almost at his feet, and vanished with a faint squeak.

'Rats,' said the dramatist. 'I'm surprised we didn't come across some before.'

He took the torch from White's hand and turned the light this way and that, examining every nook and cranny with interest.

'At one time there must have been an iron door barring this entrance we've just come through,' he said, stepping back and fingering the remnants of huge hinges. 'And this, I think, is the door itself.' He indicated an oblong object that lay on the floor in one corner, and was almost invisible under its coating of dust and grime.

Immediately opposite the passage entrance where they were standing was another arched aperture, on the other side of which the passage continued again. The iron door to this still hung on its hinges, but was wide open, just as it had been left, probably, countless years before. Lowe directed his light onto the floor and zigzagged it from side to side. The floor was composed entirely of huge flagstones, though it was difficult to make out the joins; and after a moment or two he called White's attention to the scattered footprints that were plainly visible in the layer of dirt that covered the whole floor like a film.

'Someone's been here recently,' he remarked, 'and not once, but many times.'

His secretary nodded and pointed to a dim square object that rested against the wall in the far corner. 'What's that?' he said.

Lowe went over to it. 'A perfectly good leather suitcase!' he murmured. 'I think this must be the property of our mysterious friend, the monk.'

The case was not locked, and the dramatist pressed back the spring catches. Opening the lid, he viewed the contents and nodded.

'Here's the complete outfit,' he said.

Bending forward, White saw the neatly folded black garment with its girdle and cowl. 'We seem to have struck oil this morning,' he said. 'What are you going to do about it?'

'Leave it where it is at the moment,' answered his employer. 'I think it would be bad policy to let Mr. Luckman — if it is Mr. Luckman — know that we have discovered his secret.' He closed the suitcase and put it back exactly as he had found it. 'Now,' he said, 'let's see where the rest of this passage goes to. We shouldn't be very far off from an exit of some sort.'

He proved to be correct, for they had scarcely gone more than fifty yards along the tunnel when they came to a narrow flight of stone steps that wound upwards in a spiral. They ascended carefully; and Lowe, who was counting the stairs, detected a change in the musty atmosphere when they reached the twenty-fifth. He paused and sniffed.

'Fresh air,' he said. 'We're coming out into the open.'

Another fifteen steps, and the darkness was broken by scattered rays of light. The dramatist, who was leading, saw that this filtered through a screen of leaves above him. The staircase ended here in a narrow oblong opening completely screened by thickly growing ivy.

'This is where we come out,' said Lowe. Forcing the ivy aside, he stepped from the darkness into the daylight. White followed, looking about him in surprise. They had come out by the ruined arch of the old monastery, the entrance to the passage itself being, in fact, in one of the crumbling ivy-covered walls.

'Humph! I might have guessed that this was where we should find ourselves,' remarked Lowe. 'And now I think we'll go back and see where the other side of the passage leads to.'

They re-entered the dismal place and retraced their steps. At the juncture where the roof had fallen in, they crossed over the heap of earth and stone and proceeded along the second half. This part of the tunnel was neither so straight nor in such good repair as the other, and it took a steep slope downwards. As they proceeded, the ground beneath their feet became soggy, and in places they had to splash their way through shallow pools of water. This had evidently collected from the drippings of the roof and walls.

Presently, Lowe pulled up and listened. From somewhere ahead there came the faint sound of running water. 'I think this side of the passage must come out somewhere by the river,' he said as he moved forward again. 'That's probably why it was built — to kill two birds with one stone. A secret exit from the monastery and a means of procuring water.'

They rounded a bend and saw ahead an oblong patch of light. It grew larger and clearer as they approached, and presently they came out of a small cave-like aperture close to the banks of the Loam. The entrance was concealed by a large protruding rock which made it quite impossible to detect from the sheer and almost inaccessible bank on the opposite side.

Rounding the screening rock, they found themselves standing in a sort of alcove consisting of thirty-odd square yards of rough boulder-strewn ground. Before them, the waters of the Loam raced with a faint roar over a miniature fall, while at the sides and rear a rugged natural wall rose up to a height of forty or fifty feet, in parts overgrown with bushes. Except by the secret passage, there was only one way of leaving the place and that was by the river, an unenviable task even for a good swimmer.

'This seems a nice quiet spot,' said White, looking about him.

'Nice enough and quiet enough for the person who has made use of it!' replied his employer grimly, and he pointed to something that White had not seen — a sprawling heap that lay in the shadow of a giant boulder.

'Good God!' exclaimed White. 'What is it?'

The dramatist made no reply; he was already bending over that still and motionless form and looking with set face and tightly compressed lips at the horror of the head. For the man, whoever he was, had died in the same way as Mr. William P. Ogden, and the back of his skull was not a pleasant sight.

Gently Trevor Lowe turned the body over until the livid face came into view. Then he started back with a sharp cry of astonishment, for the dead man was the motor driver — the man who in company with Murdock had so nearly been the cause of his death at the empty house in York Road!

17

The Night Alarm

Later on the same afternoon, Trevor Lowe, Inspector Shadgold, White, Inspector Jesson, and Jack and Tony were seated in the dining-room at Monk's Lodge holding a conference.

'The death of this man Blane is rather a nuisance,' said the dramatist, 'because it's impossible now for us to conceal from the killer that we know of the existence of the secret passage.'

'Why?' inquired Inspector Jesson.

'Because directly he discovers that the body's been removed, he'll naturally realise that somebody's found it!' explained Lowe dryly. 'And being a fairly sensible man, he won't use the passage anymore, which, as I've said before, is a nuisance. Had he believed that we were still ignorant of its existence, there was a fair probability that we might have caught him by setting a close watch on the place.'

'There's no reason why we shouldn't do that as it is,' said the Scotland Yard man. 'He may come back before he hears that the body's been found.'

Lowe shrugged his shoulders. 'I don't think it's probable,' he replied. 'I haven't the slightest doubt that he knows Blane's body has been found already. However much you try, you can't keep a thing like that dark in a small place like this.'

'Well, if he does come back,' put in Inspector Jesson heavily, 'he'll find trouble! I've left Finch on guard, so he won't get away again easily.'

The dramatist smiled slightly. He had nothing against Constable Finch, who was an average specimen of his class; but the idea that a rural policeman would be of the slightest use against the intelligence that they were up against amused him.

'I can't understand,' said Shadgold, frowning, 'why he left the body there. It would have been easy enough to have tipped it into the river, and then it would've drifted with the current, and it might have been days before it was discovered.'

'I don't suppose,' Lowe pointed out, 'that our murderous friend had any idea that it would be discovered where it was. He probably never anticipated that we should stumble on the secret of the underground passage. He may have intended to dispose of the body in the way you suggest, but for some reason or other — lack of time, or something like that — he postponed doing so until he paid another visit.'

'You think these two murders were committed by the same man?' asked Inspector Jesson.

Lowe nodded. 'Without question,' he replied. 'The method of killing is the same in both cases. The back of Blane's skull was crushed in almost precisely the same way as Ogden's.'

'And you believe the murderer is this man — what's his name, Luckman?' continued the local inspector.

'I think everything points that way,' said Trevor Lowe. 'That fingerprint I found proves that Luckman was in the neighbourhood at the time of Ogden's death, and this second crime makes it fairly obvious that he's still lurking about here somewhere.'

'Well, if 'e's anywhere round these parts,' remarked Inspector Jesson, ''e must be living in the woods or out in the open somewhere. I 'aven't been here long myself, but since Mr. Ogden's murder I've been making inquiries, and there aren't any strangers living in the district. Except, of course, Mr. Wyse,' he added. 'What's this man Luckman like?'

'I'm having some photographs of him sent down from the Yard,' said Shadgold. 'Though I doubt if they'll be much help to us. Luckman was rather a genius at disguise.'

'What beats me,' declared Inspector Jesson after a slight pause, 'is the meaning of all this. What's this fellow Luckman hanging about for? What did he 'ope to get out of killing Ogden and this other man?'

'We're all rather in the same boat there,' growled the Scotland Yard man. 'We don't know! The whole thing's a mystery. He seems, however, to be very interested in Monk's Lodge for some reason or other.'

Trevor Lowe might, had he cared to disclose the vague theory that was hovering at the back of his mind, have enlightened them as to Mr. Joseph Luckman's interest in the cottage. But it was only an idea, and he preferred to keep it to himself until he had succeeded in either proving or disproving it.

'What about this other man?' said Jesson. 'Murdock, you say 'is name is. It wouldn't be a bad idea to try and find 'im. If they were all working together, he could probably give us a clue to the whole business.'

'It wouldn't be a bad idea at all,' agreed Lowe, 'if you knew where to look for him! The difficulty is that he's as elusive as our friend Mr. Luckman. We know that for a short time both he and Blane made the empty house in York Road their headquarters, but where Murdock is now we haven't the least idea. One thing I'm pretty certain of, though, is that Luckman and he are not together.'

The local inspector looked surprised. 'What makes you think that, sir?' he asked.

'Because,' answered Lowe, 'although they may have worked together in the past, I'm pretty certain they're not doing so in this instance. In fact, I think the exact opposite is the case. I don't say they haven't both got the same end in view, but I think their interests are entirely distinct.'

Inspector Shadgold looked suspiciously at his friend. 'I believe you know a lot more than you have told us, Mr. Lowe,' he said gruffly.

'I assure you that I don't,' Lowe answered. 'I may guess a little more than you do, but that's a very different thing from knowing!'

'I wish you weren't so infernally close,' Shadgold grumbled. 'Why can't you say what you think and have done with it?'

'Because I'm not sure.' Lowe smiled. 'You ought to know by now, Shadgold, that I never divulge a theory of mine until I've got some solid basis of fact to go with it.'

'When will that be?' grunted Shadgold.

'Either tomorrow or the day after.'

'And what do we do in the meantime?' asked the Scotland Yard man.

'Many things,' said Lowe. 'For instance, I don't think it would do any harm to inquire into the antecedents of our friend Mr. Wyse.'

'Good God!' exclaimed Jack indignantly. 'You surely don't think he's got anything to do with it?'

'Why not?' Lowe looked across at him calmly. 'I think Wyse is an exceedingly suspicious character! His arrival in Friar's Vale coincides with the start of the peculiar happenings around here. His house is broken into one night, but certainly by no ordinary burglar, as he seemed anxious we should believe. He himself is chloroformed and the whole place turned upside down, though nothing is stolen. That in itself is sufficient to make any unprejudiced person regard him with suspicion. But in addition to that, his daughter comes up to Monk's Lodge when she imagines the place to be empty and removes something from the flowerbed.'

'She told you she wanted to look at the garden and dropped her handkerchief,' interrupted Jack.

'I know she did,' said the dramatist dryly, 'but I've yet to be convinced she was speaking the truth! My dear fellow,' he added as Jack opened his mouth to make a heated rejoinder, 'because Miss Wyse is a very attractive woman, you must not let that blind you to the fact that her actions on that afternoon were exceedingly strange. I was watching from the window and I know that it was not her handkerchief she recovered from that flowerbed!'

'And I'm prepared to swear,' grunted Jack, 'that she is perfectly innocent of any connection with this business.'

'I'm not saying she's not,' said the dramatist. 'She may have been acting purely under the dictates of her father. That Wyse knows something about this affair I'm convinced, and that's why I said it would be worth checking him up.'

'You're not suggesting that he's Luckman, are you?' said Shadgold.

'No.' Lowe shook his head. 'Neither am I saying he's not. I should merely like to know a lot more about him than I do at present, that's all.'

'I'll get through to the Yard,' said the burly inspector, 'and ask them to let us have all the information they can about him.'

'Has this man Luckman got a daughter?' asked Inspector Jesson.

'Not as far as we know,' said Shadgold, 'but I wouldn't like to say 'no' definitely. We never found out much about Luckman.

Even during the trial his past remained rather a mystery.'

'And his present seems to be in the same category,' remarked Lowe.

Inspector Jesson rose heavily to his feet. 'Well, I'm afraid I must be going, gentlemen,' he said. 'I've got a lot to do.'

'I'll walk into Friar's Vale with you,' said the Scotland Yard man. 'Then I can use the telephone at the police station to get my message through to the Yard.'

They went out together, and as soon as they had gone Jack turned to Lowe.

'I think it's a bit unfair of you, Lowe,' he said, 'to suggest ideas about Wyse like this. It may cause an awful lot of bother.'

'My dear Denton,' said the dramatist, filling his pipe, 'if Wyse is innocent, a few inquiries won't do him any harm; and if he isn't innocent, then he deserves all the harm that's coming to him.'

'Yes, but think of his daughter,' urged Jack. 'She —'

'This is a serious matter,' interrupted Lowe, 'and we can't allow sentiment to enter into it. Two brutal murders have been committed, and the man who committed them has got to answer to justice, whoever he is.'

'Yes, I suppose you're right,' admitted Jack. 'But if it should turn out to be Wyse, it will be a terrible blow for Ursula.'

'I'm afraid that will have to be risked,' said the dramatist gravely, 'and I can assure you that nobody would be more sorry for her than I.'

He lit his pipe and began to smoke thoughtfully. Presently, Tony suggested a cup of tea and went out to make it, followed by Jack.

As soon as they were alone, White turned to the dramatist. 'Do you seriously believe that Wyse is Luckman?' he asked.

'You heard what I said to Shadgold,' replied Lowe. 'I'm as much in the dark regarding Luckman's present identity as any of you.'

The meal that followed was not a particularly cheerful one. Jack was silent and morose, and Lowe appeared to be entirely occupied with his own thoughts, so that what little conversation there was, was carried on between White and Tony. As soon as tea was over, Jack left them with the plea that he had some letters to write, and went upstairs to his bedroom.

White, who was used to Lowe's moods and saw that the dramatist was anxious to be alone, suggested a walk, an offer which Tony accepted with alacrity.

It was almost completely dark when they returned, to find Lowe still sitting where they had left him, the fireplace grey with the ashes from his pipe.

He rose and stretched himself as they came in, and when Tony lit the lamp, glanced at his watch. 'By Jove,' he said, 'I had no idea it was so late! I wonder what's keeping Shadgold?'

He had scarcely made the remark when they heard the crunching of feet on the gravel outside, and a few minutes later the burly inspector came in, puffing and blowing from his long walk.

'I was just wondering what had happened to you,' said Lowe as Shadgold dropped breathlessly into a chair.

'There was a lot to do,' panted the Scotland Yard man. 'The formalities attaching to wilful murder are infinite! I've set those inquiries on foot regarding Wyse,' he added, 'and if anything can be found out about the man, we shall know in a day or so. I wish we had — what the deuce was that?'

He sprang to his feet as from outside came the sound of a shot followed by two others in rapid succession!

'Those came from an automatic!' snapped Lowe, and he sprang to the door.

As he reached the hall and was fumbling with the catch of the front door, a fourth shot split the stillness.

'They are quite close — only a few yards down the road, I should say,' panted the dramatist as he ran down the path with the others at his heels and jerked open the gate. Pausing for a moment, he peered down the narrow white ribbon of lane that showed dimly in the darkness, but he could see nothing; and then a faint groan reached his ears. He hurried forward in the direction of the sound, and had barely gone twenty yards before he stumbled over something lying at the side of the narrow path!

'Here, give me your torch, White — quickly!' he cried.

His secretary thrust it into his hand, and pressing the button, Lowe directed the light on to the huddled object at his feet.

It was Mr. Wyse, and down his left temple ran a thin trickle of blood.

18

What Does Mr. Wyse Know?

The man was not dead. The wound on his forehead was only a superficial one — a mere graze, but it would have been sufficient to stun him temporarily.

They got him back to Monk's Lodge, and by the time they had laid him on the couch in the dining room he began to show signs of returning consciousness. His eyes opened and he looked vaguely from one to the other, then raised a hand to his head.

'I shouldn't move for a moment or two, if I were you,' said Lowe as Mr. Wyse attempted to struggle to a sitting position. 'Lie still for a bit.'

The grey-haired man lay back on the cushions. 'I was attacked,' he said feebly. 'Just as I within sight of the gate. A most extraordinary affair. I can't understand it.'

'Can you tell us anything about your assailant?' Lowe asked.

'I never saw him clearly,' Wyse replied. 'It was too dark, and he had something wrapped round his face. I was coming up the lane with the intention of calling on you, when he suddenly sprang out from the cover of the hedge and fired point-blank in my face! I managed to knock his arm up so that three of the shots went wide, and then he caught me by the throat. I heard another tremendous report that nearly deafened me, and that's all I remember.'

'Can you suggest any reason for this attack?' said Lowe.

'None,' declared Mr. Wyse, his voice growing stronger as he recovered from the shock. 'It is quite inexplicable to me. I can only conclude that it was some footpad whose motive was robbery.'

'It's unusual for footpads to wander about the country with loaded revolvers,' grunted Shadgold. 'A bludgeon is generally their choice of weapon, apart from which it seems to me he chose a particularly foolish spot to lie in wait for a possible victim. The lane leads nowhere except to this cottage, and he might quite easily have waited all night without anybody passing that way at all.'

'You came in only a few minutes before we heard the shots,' said the dramatist. 'Did you see anybody lurking about?'

Shadgold shook his bullet head. 'Not a soul,' he said.

'It's most extraordinary,' said Mr. Wyse, 'but I cannot conceive any other reason for the attack.'

'You don't connect it in any way, then, with the burglary at your cottage?'

'No,' Wyse replied, 'I can't say that I do. Though now you mention it, there may possibly be a connection. Perhaps as I'm a stranger here, these scoundrels, whoever they are, imagine that I'm a wealthy man.' He smiled. 'I'm afraid that both on the occasion of the burglary, and again this time, they've been disappointed.'

'There may possibly be something in your idea,' said Lowe, and although outwardly he appeared to accept Mr. Wyse's theory, he was perfectly certain in his own mind that the man no more believed it than he did himself.

Wyse was perfectly aware of the real reason that lay behind both these incidents, and Lowe believed that he also knew the identity of the people concerned. Although apparently only one had taken part in this later development, certainly more than one had been responsible for the affair at Wyse's cottage, and he thought it not unlikely that it was Murdock and Blane who had been responsible for that episode. In that case it must have been Murdock who had shot at Wyse a short while previously. The dramatist kept these ideas to himself, however, and with the help of a first-aid case, which he fetched from his bedroom, he bound up the crime author's wound while Jack poured out a stiff glass of whisky and forced him to drink it.

'It's most kind of you — it's most kind of you,' said Mr. Wyse gratefully, setting down the empty glass. 'Except for a rather bad headache, I'm feeling better now.' He rose to his feet, but he seemed to have overestimated his own strength, for he staggered and would have fallen back on the couch but for Lowe's restraining arm.

'Without wishing to appear rude,' said

the dramatist, 'I think the best thing you can do is to return home and get to bed as soon as possible. Although the bullet has only grazed the side of your head, it's bruised the bone rather badly, and a long rest will do you good. Unless you have any particular business to do tomorrow, I shouldn't get up until late.'

'I'll take your advice,' said Mr. Wyse.

'I think I'd better see you safely on your way,' suggested Jack. 'That fellow may still be hanging about somewhere.'

'That's very kind of you — very kind of you indeed,' said the grey-haired man. 'I'm afraid I've put you all to a tremendous amount of trouble,' he added as he shook hands with Lowe and the others. 'By the way, my reason for calling on you tonight was to ask if you had made any further headway over the murder.'

'None whatever,' Lowe replied, 'except for the fact that we have now another crime to occupy our attention.'

'Another crime!' exclaimed Mr. Wyse. 'Do you mean somebody else has been killed?'

'Yes, a man called Blane,' said the

dramatist, watching the other's face narrowly as he spoke. 'He was killed in exactly the same way as Ogden was killed, which seems to show that the same person was responsible for both crimes.' He briefly explained the circumstances under which Blane's body had been discovered, and Mr. Wyse listened intently.

'Terrible — terrible!' he commented when Lowe had finished. 'And you have no clue to the identity of the murderer?'

'Not at present,' said Lowe, rather untruthfully it must be admitted, but he had no intention of acquainting Wyse with the information they had gained concerning Joseph Luckman.

'I never thought I should have the opportunity of studying a murder mystery at first hand,' remarked Mr. Wyse. 'And a secret passage, too! The whole thing might have been lifted completely from one of my own books! Most interesting!'

'Hardly so interesting to the dead men,' said Trevor Lowe.

'No — no, of course not,' agreed the grey-haired man hastily. 'I'm afraid I was allowing my enthusiasm to overcome my humanity.'

He put a few more questions, but the dramatist answered them evasively, and shortly afterward Mr. Wyse took his leave.

'What did you want to tell him anything about Blane for?' grunted Shadgold when he had gone.

'He's bound to hear about it sooner or later,' replied Lowe, 'and I rather wanted to watch his reaction to the news.'

'And what did you learn?'

'Nothing,' admitted the dramatist. 'Either he knew nothing about the crime, or he's an exceedingly good actor.'

'I should think it was the latter,' said the inspector. 'There's something very fishy about Wyse, Mr. Lowe. That whole story about a footpad and burglars wanting to rob him is rot.'

'I'm inclined to agree with you,' said Lowe thoughtfully. 'Added to which, he was lying when he said that the man fired four shots at him. Two of those shots were fired by somebody else, and I'm of the opinion that the somebody else was Wyse himself!'

'What makes you think that?' asked Shadgold.

'Well, I know all four shots didn't come from the same weapon,' explained the dramatist. 'Two came from an automatic, and two from a revolver. The difference in the sounds was obvious, and Wyse was carrying a pistol — I felt it in his pocket when he got up from the couch and staggered against me.'

Shadgold frowned. 'You know, I think we ought to have that gentleman watched,' he said. 'I believe he knows a great deal more than he ought to about what's going on around here, and he's always trying to pump us!'

'Well, he hasn't succeeded very well up to now,' said Lowe. 'And as far as watching him is concerned, I'm doubtful if it would do much good. For all his seeming simplicity, Wyse is pretty cute. Every now and then that mask of his drops, if you watch him closely enough, and the real character of the man peeps through. I don't think it would take him long to discover that someone was keeping an eye on his movements, and then you'd learn nothing. Best not to let him think we suspect him at all. If we give him enough rope, he'll hang himself.'

'More likely the public executioner will do it for him!' said Shadgold. 'I wonder if he *is* Luckman.'

'There is a perfectly simple way of finding that out,' said the dramatist, 'and that's to get hold of one of his fingerprints and compare it with the mark I found on the paint.'

'By Jove, yes!' said the Scotland Yard man. 'I wonder I didn't think of that. That would settle it definitely one way or the other.'

They went on discussing the case, and it was well past midnight before they finally went to their respective rooms.

There was a letter for Trevor Lowe in the morning bearing the Dryseley postmark, and after he had read it he announced his intention of going out directly after breakfast.

The others were in the middle of lunch when he returned, and White could tell by Lowe's appearance that he had discovered something. He said nothing, however, until the meal had been cleared away and Tony and Jack had gone out, and then with his pipe well alight he looked across at Shadgold and White.

'I told you some time back,' he said, 'that I had a theory concerning the motive at the back of this business, and that when I had confirmed it you should know what it was. Well, I partly confirmed it this morning.'

'Let's hear it,' Shadgold said shortly.

'When I went over to Dryseley the other day, I paid a visit to the estate office that Ogden used to run and had a chat with Wishart, his managing clerk. As you know, this cottage belongs to some people called Cheply who are at present in America. I was rather anxious, however, to find out if there'd been a previous owner, and I got Wishart to cable the Cheplys for permission to have a look at their title deeds or lease. That letter I got this morning was from Wishart to say that he'd got the necessary permission, and in order save time had had copies of the documents in question sent by the Cheplys' solicitors to his office.'

He paused and sucked thoughtfully at his pipe.

'Monk's Lodge did have a previous owner.'

'Who?' demanded White.

'Joseph Luckman.'

'What?' Shadgold bounded from his

chair as though something had stung him. 'Are you sure of that?'

'Yes. There's no shadow of doubt,' Lowe said. 'His signature appears twice on those documents.'

'By Jove, that's a useful discovery, Mr. Lowe!' Shadgold exclaimed. 'It supplies the link we've been looking for — the link between Luckman and this cottage.'

'It does more than that,' said Trevor Lowe. 'When I tell you that the date upon which these documents were signed, transferring the lease of Monk's Lodge to the Cheplys, was three weeks after the Hatton Garden robbery, and one week before Luckman was arrested, you'll see that it supplies a fairly good reason for his being in the neighbourhood at present.'

'I don't follow you.' Shadgold frowned.

'You will in a minute,' replied Lowe. 'When Luckman was arrested and brought up for trial on the charge of murder, so much importance was attached to the major offence that the secondary part of his criminal act didn't receive much attention. In short, the robbery rather faded into the background in comparison.'

'Not with the firm who suffered!' said Shadgold dryly.

'Possibly not,' the dramatist resumed, 'but I'm talking about the general public and the police at the moment. The result was that when Luckman said he'd thrown the diamonds into the Thames, he was more or less believed.'

'We had men dragging the place for days,' grunted the inspector.

'But you never found them,' snapped Lowe quickly, 'and that's the whole point of my theory! I don't believe Luckman ever did throw those stones into the river. I believe he knew that the police were after him, and having already prepared his plea of insanity in case he should be caught, hid the diamonds for the time when he'd be free to recover them.'

'You mean —' began White excitedly.

'I mean that somewhere in the neighbourhood of Monk's Lodge is a hundred thousand pounds' worth of diamonds, and Luckman is here because he wants to get hold of them!'

19

Mr. Wyse Acts Strangely

There was a long silence following Lowe's last words, while White and Shadgold stared at him, and then the inspector brought his fist down on the table with a thud that shook the whole cottage.

'Mr. Lowe, I believe you've hit it!' he exclaimed. 'He's after those diamonds! That would account for the warning on the window and all the other tricks. He wants the cottage empty. They're hidden somewhere in this house.'

'I think you're wrong there, Shadgold,' Lowe disagreed. 'I don't think the diamonds are hidden in this house at all. If they were, he could've got them easily enough before I came down. Denton and Frost were out for hours at a stretch. There would have been plenty of time for him to have slipped in and removed them from their hiding place. No, there's something more in it than that!

I firmly believe that it's necessary for him to get this place empty before he can lay his hands on those stones, but *why* it's necessary has me stumped.'

'Perhaps he's bricked them up somewhere in the walls,' suggested White.

Lowe shook his head. 'He'd know whereabouts they were; and even in that case he would have had plenty of time to get them. No; whatever the clue to the whereabouts of those diamonds is, it entails the spending of a lengthy period in this house. Longer than the opportunity offered by a few hours' absence of the tenants would allow.'

'But why then should he have transferred his lease to the Cheplys at all?' Shadgold said. 'He might have foreseen this complication. If they'd never gone to America at all, he would have been in the same difficulty, only in that case they would've been living here themselves.'

'No, they wouldn't,' said the dramatist. 'Wishart told me it was their habit to spend three months away every summer — at least, that's what they told him when they took possession, though they weren't here long enough to put it into actual practice.

Some alterations in their plan necessitated them going to America. However, I've no doubt that this projected three months' absence every year was known to Luckman when he transferred the property. Probably it was the inducement that made him choose the Cheplys. As for the reason why he didn't keep the place himself, that seems to me fairly obvious. With somebody else living here, the police were unlikely to connect Luckman with the place, even if they should suspect that the diamonds were not at the bottom of the river — which, apparently, they did not.'

'Continuing on the lines of your theory, then,' said Shadgold, 'Luckman must have come down here immediately after the robbery, concealed the diamonds somewhere, and then arranged to lease the place to the Cheplys?'

'That's correct,' agreed Lowe. 'He knew that it would be hopeless trying to dispose of them right away, and he'd made up his mind that, if he was arrested, he would swear he'd thrown them in the Thames. This assertion on his part would certainly help him with his plea of insanity, for no one in their right senses would go to the length of murder to obtain a hundred thousand pounds' worth of diamonds and then throw them away, which is practically what Luckman admitted having done.'

'You're quite right,' said the Scotland Yard man. 'That was one of the main arguments for the defence. Luckman's counsel said that if he'd thrown the stones away after he'd been arrested — which, of course, it was proved he couldn't have done — it would've been a different matter. But to have thrown them away before he had any inkling that the police were on his track proved that his mind must be seriously unbalanced. Those were not his exact words, but that's the gist of what he said.'

'I think he was right,' said the dramatist. 'And I think the doctors were right to a certain extent when they certified that Luckman was insane. There's not a shadow of a doubt that the man is mentally unbalanced, but I entirely disagree that he's not responsible for his actions. He's mad, and has the cunning of a madman, without the meaningless actions of a lunatic.'

'How do you suppose Murdock and

Blane come into this?' asked White.

'I should say that they were here for the same purpose as Luckman himself,' replied Lowe after a moment's thought. 'They helped him with the robbery, and I've no doubt were promised a share of the proceeds. Luckman probably double-crossed them. He may or he may not have told them of the existence of this cottage, but I don't think he told them the diamonds were hidden here. Possibly he hoped they'd believe his story about throwing them in the river. Somehow or other, however, they must have discovered for themselves, and that's what brought them down here.'

'Well, we certainly seem to be a good step nearer,' said Shadgold cheerfully.

Lowe smiled. 'You mustn't forget,' he pointed out, 'that most of this is pure conjecture. The only actual facts we've got in our possession are that a hundred thousand pounds' worth of diamonds were stolen; that Joseph Luckman is somewhere in the neighbourhood; that Murdock and Blane were also in the neighbourhood, and that Murdock probably still is; and that Luckman was the original owner of Monk's Lodge.'

'All the same,' said the Scotland Yard man, 'I think your theory's pretty near the truth, although it doesn't account for Ogden's murder.'

'No, but it suggests a motive. Supposing Ogden, on his way up to the cottage to keep that appointment, saw Luckman and recognised him? That would supply a reason for his death.'

'Yes.' The inspector nodded his head quickly. 'Well, it seems the next thing we've got to do is find Luckman.'

Lowe rose and, crossing to the mantel-piece, knocked out the ashes of his pipe. 'That,' he answered, 'is, I think, a question of patience. Sooner or later, if I'm correct, Luckman will give himself away.'

'I hope it'll be sooner,' grunted Shadgold, and he changed the subject as Jack and Tony came in.

Almost immediately after tea, Shadgold announced his intention of going down to the police station to see Inspector Jesson. Since the evening was a fine one and there was nothing just then to occupy their attention, Lowe and White suggested a walk, and invited one of the other two to come with them. It had been arranged that someone should always stay on guard at the cottage, so Jack and Tony tossed up for it, and won.

'Off you go!' said Jack with a grin. 'I'll remain and defend the castle.'

He waved them a cheery farewell and began to clear away the tea. He was in the midst of washing up when there came a knock at the front door. Upon opening it, to his astonishment he saw Ursula Wyse standing on the threshold.

'I hope I'm not disturbing you,' she said, 'but I was going for a walk, and Father asked me if I'd bring this note to Mr. Lowe.'

Jack became suddenly acutely conscious of the fact that he was in his shirt sleeves. 'They're all out at the moment,' he said. 'Won't you come in?'

She stepped into the hall, and he led her to the dining room. 'Do sit down,' he said hurriedly. 'I won't be a moment!' And, dashing into the kitchen, he retrieved his jacket. 'Now,' he said when he had returned, 'being clothed and in my right mind, we can talk. How's your father feeling after last night?'

'His head still hurts him, but otherwise he's quite all right,' Ursula replied.

'Do you know any reason why your father should have been attacked?'

'No — but is there any reason for anything that's happening round here?' she replied.

Jack noticed that she had evaded giving a direct answer. 'I suppose there must be a reason if we only knew what it was,' he said. 'There's a reason for everything, unless of course you're dealing with a lunatic.'

She gave a little smothered cry and the colour drained from her face. 'Why do you say that?' she whispered nervously.

'I don't know.' He was astonished at the effect of his words. 'I didn't mean to frighten you. But under the circumstances it seems the most natural conclusion to come to, doesn't it?'

'Does — does Mr. Lowe think that too?' she asked, still in the same low, almost inaudible voice.

'I don't know what Trevor Lowe thinks,'

said Jack. 'He's rather good at keeping his thoughts to himself.'

Ursula sat for a moment in silence, then: 'I wish you'd try to do something for me,' she said suddenly.

'I will if I can,' he replied.

She leaned forward and laid her hand on his arm. 'Go away from Monk's Lodge,' she said earnestly. 'And persuade the others to go away, too.'

'That's the second time you've suggested that,' Jack said. 'Why?'

'Because something dreadful will happen if you don't, and I'm afraid! Oh, you don't know how afraid I am!'

Jack looked every bit as surprised as he felt. 'Don't you think,' he said gently, 'that you're rather letting your nerves get the better of you? It's quite understandable, of course — I mean after the burglary at your place, and the attack on your father and all the rest of it. But even if I wanted to run away from here, which I don't, it would be impossible to persuade the others to go. Detective-Inspector Shadgold is here officially to inquire into the murder of poor Ogden, and until he's completed his job he'll stop here. Only the fact that he was recalled by Scotland Yard would alter that.'

'I suppose I am being rather stupid,' she admitted, and then glancing at the watch on her wrist, she hurriedly added: 'I must go now. Father will be wondering what has happened to me.'

She rose to her feet, and Jack felt rather in a quandary. It was impossible to let Ursula go by herself. But Lowe's instructions had been implicit: Monk's Lodge was not to be left untenanted for any length of time, and it was his duty to stay in the place. He had to decide quickly, and he decided on a compromise.

'I'll come with you as far as the end of the lane,' he said, and she thanked him.

The man who had been watching the cottage from the shadow of the wood smiled to himself as he saw them pass out of the little gate, and as they walked slowly down the winding lane that led away from Monk's Lodge he began to make his way stealthily across the lawn.

Ursula made no further allusion to her fears, but chatted gaily on varying subjects until Jack said goodbye to her at the place where the lane joined the main road. He watched her until she disappeared into the gathering dusk, and then, turning, retraced his steps to the cottage. He sincerely hoped that none of the others had come back while he had been away from his post. Not that he thought the short half-hour, which it had taken him to walk down the lane and back again, would make much difference, but he did not want them to think he could not be trusted to remain in the place.

He was still trying to justify to himself this rank neglect of his duty when he reached the gate of Monk's Lodge, and he was just going to push it open when a gleam of light flashing momentarily from the dining room window attracted his attention. So the others must have come back during his absence, thought Jack. They could not have been back so very long, or they would have lighted the lamp. The flash of light he had seen had been more like the striking of a match. If he slipped quietly up the path and onto the lawn, he might pretend that he had merely been in the garden for a smoke.

He put this plan into execution, and reaching the lawn approached the open window. Peering in, he saw somebody over by the opposite wall. Thinking that it was one of the others, he was in the act of making his presence known when the white ray of a torch flashed out, and in the light Jack caught sight of the bandage round the man's head. It was Mr. Wyse!

Jack stood motionless, staring in utter astonishment. To find Mr. Wyse in the house at all just then was remarkable enough, but his actions were even more remarkable. For by the light of his torch, Mr. Wyse was engaged in washing the whitewashed wall with a large sponge, the water for which was supplied from a basin that stood on the floor by his side!

20

Lowe's Plan

For the moment Jack thought he was suffering from a delusion, but there was no doubt about it — Mr. Wyse was there; and even as Jack continued to gaze in stupefied astonishment, the grey-haired man bent down and squeezed the sponge out into the basin of water.

He was in the act of recommencing his washing operations, and Jack was trying to make up his mind whether or not he should make his presence known, when there came a click from the gate and the sound of voices. The others had come back. Instantly the torch that Mr. Wyse was holding went out, and Jack heard a hurried movement inside the cottage.

Leaving the window, Jack went quickly towards the little path and met Trevor Lowe, White and Tony just as they reached the front door.

'Who's that?' asked Lowe sharply as his figure loomed out of the gloom.

'It's me, Denton,' whispered Jack. 'Don't make a noise. Wyse is inside and he's behaving in a most extraordinary manner!'

'Wyse? What's he doing?'

'Washing the wall,' said Jack. 'He's got a sponge and water.'

'Open the door quickly,' Lowe said softly, and Jack fumbled for his key.

They entered the little hall and stopped for a moment, listening. Not a sound greeted them from the interior of the cottage, and going towards the open door of the dining room Lowe peered in. The room was in darkness and there was certainly nobody there. 'Light the lamp,' he said over his shoulder to Tony, and entered.

There came the scrape of a match and then, as Tony applied it to the wick of the lamp, the gloom was dissipated. The yellow light glistened on a patch of wetness on the wall by the fireplace, and, going over, Lowe looked at it closely. The distemper was not of the washable kind and had run down in streaks over the oak panelling below, and where Mr. Wyse's sponge had been at work was an irregular expanse of bare plaster. And that was all! Although the dramatist examined the place closely, he could find neither crack nor mark to account for the spoiling of the wall.

Turning from his scrutiny of the damage, he looked across at Jack. 'How was it that he managed to get in and do this without you knowing anything about it?' he asked.

'I — I went out,' Jack answered. 'You see, Ursula — er — Miss Wyse called soon after you'd gone. As a matter of fact, she brought a note for you from her father, and I — well I couldn't very well let her go back alone, it was getting dusk and — I didn't know whether that fellow who attacked Wyse might still be hanging about and so I —'

'So you saw her home?' interrupted Lowe.

'Not all the way,' said Jack hurriedly. 'Only as far as the end of the lane.'

'I see.' The dramatist frowned thoughtfully. 'Where's this note you were talking about?'

Jack produced it from his pocket and held it out. Lowe took it and, ripping open the envelope, withdrew the sheet of paper it contained. He read the few lines scrawled across it and smiled.

'Dear Mr. Lowe,' ran the note, 'I have a theory in connection with the murder at Monk's Lodge that I should like to discuss with you. Perhaps you could drop in and see me sometime. P. Wyse.'

'A very clever idea to get rid of you,' he said, tossing the note across to Jack. 'Mr. Wyse seems to be a most ingenious person. He sent his daughter with this note, being practically certain that you wouldn't let her go back alone, and that he'd therefore have the cottage to himself for sufficient time to enable him to carry out his experiment on the wall. I have no doubt he imagined that you'd see Ursula right home, instead of leaving her at the bottom of the lane, in which case he would've been gone before you got back.'

'But how in the world did he know we'd gone out?' broke in White.

'Most probably because he was watching and saw us go,' Lowe replied. 'He then scribbled the note, which you can see has been done very hastily in pencil, and gave it to his daughter to deliver.'

'Then she must have been with him,' said his secretary.

'Oh, yes. I've very little doubt she was with him,' agreed Lowe. 'Her job was to induce Denton to see her home. I expect she mentioned something about being frightened after the attack on her father or something of the sort.' He looked inquiringly across at Jack, who appeared rather uncomfortable.

'As a matter of fact she did,' he admitted reluctantly. 'She wanted me to persuade you all to leave the cottage. Said she knew something terrible would happen if we remained, and that she was horribly frightened.'

'Exactly what I thought,' Lowe said.

Jack went on quickly: 'But she can't be in this business. She can't know anything about it.'

Trevor Lowe looked at him steadily. 'I wonder if you'd be so certain of that if Ursula Wyse was fat and ugly,' he remarked. 'I'm sorry to disillusion you, Denton, but I'm of the opinion that that young lady knows as much about this business as Wyse himself.'

'The question is, *what* does he know about it?' said White.

'Apparently a good deal more than we do,' replied Lowe. 'He wouldn't have gone to all this trouble —' He nodded towards the damp patch. '—just because he didn't like the colour of the distemper on the wall.'

'It seems a mad thing to do, to me,' muttered Tony. 'What possible object could he have?'

'Whatever it was,' answered Lowe evasively, 'I have no doubt it was a very good one.'

The sound of heavy steps crunching on the gravel outside stopped him going on, and a moment later Shadgold came in.

'Hello!' he greeted them, throwing his hat onto the sofa. 'I've got those photographs of Luckman. They've just arrived from the Yard.'

He laid a large envelope he had been carrying on the table and took out several prints. The others crowded round him as he held them fanwise in his fingers. There were half a dozen of them, and they were the photographs of a man taken in various positions. There were two profiles, left and right, a full face, and three full lengths.

The notorious Joseph Luckman was a middle-aged man with a smooth, expressionless face, and a head that was almost totally devoid of hair. His eyes were vacant and revealed no character at all. It was the sort of face that no one would look at twice.

'Unpleasant-looking fellow, isn't he?' remarked the inspector as Lowe took the photographs from his hand and scrutinised them one by one intently.

'How many copies of these have you got?' asked the dramatist.

'Only those,' replied Shadgold. 'Why?'

Without answering, Lowe turned to White. 'Did you bring your photographic oufit with you?'

'Yes, I thought there might be some good pictures to pick up here.'

Lowe held out the full-face picture of Luckman. 'Do you think you could make a dozen copies of this?'

'Yes, I think so,' answered White. 'It shouldn't be difficult. When do you want them?'

'As soon as you can do them.'

'I'll have them ready in two hours,'

replied White, and taking the photographs he hurried out of the room.

'What's the idea?' demanded Shadgold.

'Rather a good one, I think,' answered Lowe. 'It occurred to me while I was looking at those photographs. I'll tell you all about it later. In the meanwhile, I should like to hear what you make of this.' He gave the Scotland Yard man a brief account of the queer behaviour of Mr. Wyse, and Shadgold listened with undisguised astonishment.

'What do you think the idea was?' mused the inspector.

'I should think,' said Lowe, 'that Wyse was trying to find where those diamonds are.'

'You mean that he's Luckman?' said Shadgold quickly.

'He may be,' said Lowe, 'or he may not be. Whoever he is, however, I'm convinced that those diamonds are at the bottom of his strange behaviour.'

Jack and Tony, who had been looking rather mystified ever since Shadgold had come in, exchanged glances, and Jack put their combined thoughts into words.

'Look here!' he said. 'Who is Luckman, and what are these diamonds you're talking about?'

'Luckman,' replied Lowe, 'is a gentleman who ended his nefarious career of crime by breaking into a diamond merchant's in Hatton Garden and stealing a hundred thousand pounds' worth of diamonds after murdering the night watchman. He wasn't hanged as he ought to have been, but was certified insane and sent to Broadmoor, from whence he succeeded in escaping a few weeks ago.'

'But why should he be mixed up in this business?' asked Tony. 'Why do you think the diamonds are here?'

'Because this cottage once belonged to Luckman,' said Lowe, and he told them of his discoveries to date.

'Well, we certainly seem to be getting to the bottom of it at last,' remarked Tony as Lowe concluded. 'But I don't see how Wyse expected to find the diamonds by washing the wall. Surely he didn't believe they were concealed beneath the distemper?'

'Hardly!' said Lowe with a slight smile. 'But I think he was hoping to find some clue that would tell him where they actually are hidden.'

'What?' demanded Shadgold.

'As I don't happen to be a thought-reader, retorted Lowe, 'I really can't tell you.'

They could get no more out of him than that, and Tony and Jack went off to get supper, leaving Shadgold pacing restlessly up and down the room and Lowe sitting thoughtfully smoking in the armchair.

The meal had long been over when White made a reappearance. 'Those photographs are all ready for you,' he announced. 'I've put them between some sheets of blotting-paper to dry.'

'Excellent,' said the dramatist, rising to his feet. 'Where have you put them?'

'In your bedroom,' answered his secretary as he seated himself at the table and looked round to see what there was left to eat.

'Then I think, if you'll excuse me,' said Lowe, crossing to the door, 'I'll leave you all.' He nodded and went out.

White looked over at Shadgold. 'What's in the wind? Do you know?' he asked, with his mouth full.

'I don't know anything!' growled the inspector. 'All I know is that Mr. Lowe can be darned exasperating at times. He's got some idea at the back of his mind, but I suppose as usual we shall have to wait with as much patience as we can until he's ready to let us hear it.'

They would still have been mystified had they been able to see what Lowe was doing at that particular moment; for, having reached his bedroom and drawn the curtains, he seated himself at the small table on which the photographic prints lay drying and began carefully to sharpen a number of pencils which he had taken out of his suitcase. When he had done this, he studied the prints one by one. They were still slightly damp, and he laid them aside to dry thoroughly.

Presently he found that they were dry enough for his purpose, and began to work on the long and curious task which he had set himself. He heard the others come up to bed and the house settle into silence, and still he worked on. The birds were twittering in the trees and the first pale yellow rays of the rising sun were filtering through the gap in the curtains before he finally rose stiffly and stretched himself. He looked tired and haggard, but there was a gleam in his eyes that betokened satisfaction as he picked up the prints that littered the table and locked them carefully away in his suitcase.

By the time he had had a cold bath and shaved, the sound of sizzling bacon told him that breakfast was being prepared. He went downstairs and greeted the others with a cheerful 'good morning'; and then, as White handed him a cup of coffee, he exploded his bombshell.

'What was it you told me Miss Wyse said last night?' he asked, addressing Jack.

The young man looked surprised. 'She suggested that I should try and persuade you all to leave, if that's what you mean,' said Jack.

'That's what I mean,' said Lowe, 'and I think her advice is excellent.'

'What!' Shadgold, who was in the act of drinking his coffee, nearly choked himself.

'I've been thinking it over,' said Lowe, 'and I think her advice is so good that I've decided to take it.'

'Look here! What are you talking about?' demanded Shadgold.

'I thought I'd put my meaning into plain English,' said the dramatist. 'I have every intention of leaving Monk's Lodge today, and if you'll take my advice you'll all come with me!'

They stared at him, too utterly astonished to say a word.

21

A Call on Mr. Wyse

The following morning, Trevor Lowe's big car with White at the wheel came to a halt outside the cottage occupied by Mr. Wyse and his daughter.

'I shan't be long,' said the dramatist as he got out, and Shadgold nodded.

'Can I come with you?' asked Jack with a lamentable attempt at unconcern.

'By all means.' Lowe smiled.

Jack was out of the car almost before he had finished speaking. As they walked up the tiny path, the front door was opened and Mr. Wyse himself appeared on the threshold with a beaming smile.

'This is an unexpected pleasure,' he said. 'Come in, come in.' He led the way into the sitting-room and waved them into comfortable chairs. 'My daughter will be sorry to have missed you,' he went on.

'She's gone over to King's Hayling to do some shopping.'

Jack's face fell.

'How's your head, Mr. Wyse?' Lowe asked.

The author of crime stories raised his hand and touched the profusion of white bandage that was swathed about his forehead like a miniature turban. 'It's much better, thank you,' he replied. 'Except that it rather disturbs my rest, and I still have a headache.'

'You ought to get your doctor to prescribe something for that,' said Lowe sympathetically. 'A mild opiate, perhaps.'

Mr. Wyse seated himself at the table. 'As a matter of fact, I was considering running up to town this week to see my own doctor,' he said. 'I haven't much faith in these local men.' He changed the topic of conversation. 'How are things going at Phantom Hollow? Any fresh developments?'

'As a matter of fact, Mr. Wyse,' said Lowe, 'we're leaving Monk's Lodge today.'

'Leaving Monk's Lodge today!' Wyse echoed, getting to his feet. 'For how long?'

'For good,' said Lowe. 'We've talked it

over and come to the conclusion that we're only wasting our time.'

'Dear me.' Mr. Wyse was a little breathless. 'This is surely a very sudden decision?'

'I'm afraid I am rather an erratic person.' Lowe smiled. 'And I have a lot of work awaiting me in London. So really this visit is partly in the nature of a farewell.'

'Partly?' Mr. Wyse raised his eyebrows.

'I must confess that I had another reason for calling,' Lowe said. 'As an author of crime stories, you must naturally possess a great many of the attributes of a detective yourself.'

'I have a certain amount of experience in thinking on those lines,' Wyse admitted modestly, 'if not in any practical way.'

'Exactly,' said Lowe. 'And so I've come to ask you, purely out of professional curiosity, that if you were writing a story about the situation that has actually happened at Monk's Lodge, what explanation you would give?'

'That,' said Mr. Wyse, frowning, 'is a big question. In the first place, I should endeavour to write nothing ordinary. I should endeavour to evolve a solution that was as unexpected as possible, while at the same time keeping it simple.'

'And there's where we come up against the difference between fiction and real life,' remarked Lowe as the other paused. 'Your real-life explanation, while nearly always being simple, is quite expected.'

Mr. Wyse looked suddenly interested. 'Are you suggesting,' he said, 'that the explanation of the murder of Ogden bears out that idea?'

'So far as that's concerned,' Lowe replied, 'I can't venture an opinion since I am, to be quite frank, quite unable to see any explanation at all. I was speaking generally.'

'To a certain extent I agree with you,' said Mr. Wyse thoughtfully. 'Real-life crime is nearly always sordid. A man or a woman is murdered, and it nearly always turns out that the person most suspected is the guilty party. Police work consists for the most part of patient and monotonous enquiries to find sufficient evidence for a conviction, not in discovering the identity of the murderer. But —' He smiled and shrugged his shoulders. '—in fiction, as in the drama, we have to take a slice of real life and dress it so as to make it palatable for the public to digest. Real life is very crude, Mr. Lowe, as you know, and most people have sufficient of it in their own lives without wishing to read about it or see it on the stage. They want something that will take their minds off the worries and cares they encounter daily, not enhance them.' He laughed a little apologetically. 'You must forgive,' he said, 'but you've got me on my hobby horse.'

'I not only forgive you, but I agree with you,' said Lowe. 'I believe you said that you've had nothing as yet published?'

'Unfortunately that's true,' murmured Mr. Wyse regretfully.

'I was wondering whether I could help you,' said Lowe. 'I number quite a few publishers among my personal friends, and perhaps if you'd let me have one of your manuscripts to read, I might be able to do something.'

'I should be delighted,' said Mr. Wyse.

'Then if you'll look one out, I'll take it with me,' said the dramatist, glancing at his watch. 'I must be going very shortly. I have to drop in and see Inspector Jesson.'

Mr. Wyse looked really embarrassed. He

coughed and fidgeted, and at last spoke: 'I
— I should like to read through the — er
— story before — er — submitting it for
your criticism,' he stammered. 'I — you see
—'

'Oh, that doesn't matter,' said Lowe
quickly. 'What I want to do is to get some
idea of your style. You could, of course, have
it back to make any corrections before I
placed it in the hands of anybody else.'

'It's most kind of you.' Mr. Wyse's em-
barrassment was increasing by leaps and
bounds. 'But really — if you don't mind
I — er — I would rather send it to you. I
should like to have time to make the best
selection.'

'All right, if you prefer,' said Lowe. 'My
address is in the telephone book.' He rose
to his feet. 'And now I really must go. I'm
delighted to have met you, Mr. Wyse, and
I hope I can be of assistance to you.'

The grey-haired man shook his out-
stretched hand. Ushering them to the door,
he stood and watched them go down the
path to the waiting car.

'Why did you ask him to let you have one
of his stories?' asked Jack as they got in.

'Because I never expected to get one,' answered Lowe. 'I should have been very much surprised if Mr. Wyse had produced a story in any form except from his lips. For I doubt very much if he's ever written anything longer than a letter in his life.'

Jack relapsed into silence and wondered.

* * *

Back in the comfortable sitting-room of his cottage, Mr. Wyse was staring at the ceiling and wondering, too. 'Now, I wonder exactly what the game is?' he muttered aloud after a long cogitation. 'That man's up to something. What is it?'

He spent the rest of the day trying to satisfy himself, but without result, and he was worried, for he took a professional interest in the doings of Trevor Lowe.

22

Lowe Suggests a Retreat

Inspector Jesson sat in his small, dingy office, staring thoughtfully through the little window at a cow that was grazing in a field close by. But it is doubtful whether he even saw the cow, for his mental energies were entirely concentrated on Monk's Lodge.

He was still staring out of the window when the sound of voices from the charge-room adjoining reached his ears, and he looked up as he recognised the rather gruff tones of one of the men he had been thinking about. There was a tap on the door, and in answer to his invitation it opened, and Trevor Lowe and Shadgold came in.

'Good morning,' said the dramatist genially.

'Good morning,' said Inspector Jesson, and he wondered as he glanced at the clock what the reason for this early visit could be.

'We've just come in to say goodbye to

you,' went on Lowe. 'Inspector Shadgold and I are catching the eleven-five from King's Hayling.'

'Where to?' asked Inspector Jesson in astonishment.

'To London,' replied the dramatist. 'To tell you the truth, Inspector, I've been talking the matter over with my friends, and we've come to the conclusion that it's useless remaining in the district any longer. There's absolutely no motive either for the murder of Ogden or the other man, Blane. We're fairly certain that the crimes were committed by Luckman, and since we know him to be insane, it's a sheer waste of time to look for a motive that doesn't exist. He may or may not still be in the neighbourhood; it's impossible to say. But his capture now is purely a matter of routine work by the police. Inspector Shadgold, I need hardly add, entirely agrees with me, and is making his report to Scotland Yard on those lines.'

Inspector Jesson was recovering slowly from his first astonishment. 'Will you be seeing the chief constable before you go, sir?' he asked, addressing Shadgold.

The Scotland Yard man nodded. 'Yes, I think there'll just be time to have a word with him.'

Lowe glanced at the clock. 'In that case, we'd better be going now,' he said. 'Goodbye, Jesson. Oh, and by the way, you might say goodbye to Dr. McGuire for me. Explain the circumstances to him and say that I hadn't time myself.'

'I will,' said the inspector, and he accompanied them to the door of the police station. Lowe's car, with White at the wheel and Jack and Tony at the back, was drawn up by the kerb, and when Lowe and Shadgold had taken their places it moved slowly off in the direction of King's Hayling.

Inspector Jesson stood and watched until it vanished in the distance; then, going back to his little office, he shut the door and, sitting down at his desk, fixed his eyes once more upon the grazing cow.

★   ★   ★

Night gathered slowly round Monk's Lodge. It came up stealthily, heralded by long shadows and heavy, angry-looking storm clouds

261

that hung low over the horizon into which the setting sun sank and was drowned. The air grew chill as a faint breeze stirred the tops of the trees and set them whispering.

The long spell of fine weather had broken at last. Away to the south a jagged ribbon of blue fire split the heavy bank of cloud, and long afterwards there came a dull muttering rumble as though the earth were grumbling at this attack from the sky. As suddenly as it had arisen, the breeze dropped, and the whole countryside became still and silent — a curious stillness and silence, rather as though it were listening. No sound of bird or animal broke that oppressive stillness; and then, that which all nature seemed to be waiting for, came.

With a hissing, rending roar, the storm broke. A sudden culminating crash of deafening noise muttered and rolled away into silence, followed, as though that had been the signal for which they had been waiting, by the wind and the rain.

It beat at the face of the man who, with bowed head, was walking rapidly up the winding lane, stinging his skin and blinding his eyes so that he found vision difficult. But he came on, splashing his way through the miniature river that swirled at his feet. He was scarcely visible in the darkness, for he wore a long black coat that reached almost to his heels, and his soft hat was pulled low over his forehead.

He reached the little gate leading into the garden of Monk's Lodge, and pushing it open made his way up the path to the front door. In the shelter of the porch he shook the water from his coat and hat, and then taking something from his pocket he bent down and began to work methodically on the lock. At the expiration of five minutes there was a faint click, and the door swung gently open under pressure.

Entering the room, he went across to the window and drew the curtains, then going back to the door shut it and stood for some moments looking at it. Next he took a large bottle from his pocket and set it down on the floor, then arranged his torch on the table so that its light fell fully on the painted surface of the door.

There was a large, shallow bowl on the sideboard, and, fetching this across, he poured into it the contents of the bottle.

From his inside breast pocket he produced a sponge, and dipping this into the mixture in the bowl, he proceeded to rub vigorously at the paintwork of the door. He did not attempt to cover the entire surface, but confined his attentions to a space about two feet square that was almost level with his eyes.

He worked swiftly and methodically, stooping every now and again to re-moisten the sponge. At first there was very little show for his labours, but presently the strong fluid began to take effect and the smooth surface of the paint became rough and dull.

An hour passed; two hours; and still he continued tirelessly rubbing the sponge in small circular sweeps. It was nearly four hours later before he apparently completed his task to his satisfaction. The entire paint-ed surface had been removed in a ragged square. Dropping the sponge in the bowl, he stepped over to the table and, bringing the torch back to the door, directed its light on the place at which he had been working.

Now that the covering film of paint had been removed, several black markings were visible on the wood beneath. The intruder allowed a little exclamation of satisfaction to escape his lips; and then, taking a notebook and pencil from his pocket, he proceeded to copy the wavering lines on the panel. When this was done, he returned the book and pencil, replaced the torch on the table, and once more set to work with the sponge, quickly obliterating the inscription which his labours had brought to light.

'I think that will do,' he murmured at last.

'I think so, too, Luckman!' cried a voice from the door.

The man in the long coat swung round, the sponge still gripped in his hand, and his teeth bared in a snarl of astonishment and fear.

Trevor Lowe stood on the threshold, the blunt nose of the automatic he held glinting in the reflected light of the torch. 'Put up your hands,' said the dramatist quickly, 'and don't try any tricks, because I shan't hesitate to shoot!'

Luckman remained motionless for a second and then began slowly to raise his arms. Lowe took a step forward, followed by the shadowy form of Shadgold, but as he moved the man in the long coat acted. With a sudden sharp flick of his wrist, he flung the sponge in the dramatist's face. It caught Lowe just between the eyes, and the strong soda pickle with which it was drenched momentarily blinded him.

'Look out, Shadgold!' he cried, and pressed the trigger of his pistol.

The noise of the shots was deafening in the confined space of the room, but Luckman was no longer on the spot where Lowe had aimed. At the same instant the sponge had left his hand, he had sprung aside towards the torch and, the next second, had switched it off, plunging the room into darkness.

'White — Shadgold — don't let him get away!' cried Lowe, dabbing at his smarting eyes with a handkerchief.

The Scotland Yard man grunted a reply and sprang forward, followed by White, but he could see nothing in that pitch blackness, and there came a crash of glass and a draught of cold wind.

'He's gone through the window,' said the dramatist. 'Go on, after him!' He stumbled across the room, cannoning into tables and chairs.

'There he goes!' exclaimed White. 'Running across the lawn!' Heedless of the splintered glass that tore his clothes and cut his hands, he swung himself through the broken window and went off in pursuit. Pausing only to fling up the sash, Inspector Shadgold scrambled after him, with Lowe but a few paces in the rear.

The storm had passed, and the fitful light of a watery moon was sufficient to show the dim figure of Luckman for a second, just before it vanished into the shadow of the hedge.

'He's making for the wood,' panted White as he forced his way through the thicket. 'We shall lose him if we're not careful!'

They saw their quarry for a moment as he dodged between the tree trunks, and then he was lost in a patch of heavy shadow.

'He's turned off to the right,' said Shadgold jerkily as he drew up level with White. 'Look — there he is,' he added a moment after, 'going towards the ruins of the old monastery!'

They changed their direction and went

crashing through the undergrowth in the fugitive's wake, but when they reached the ruins there was no sign of him. They paused for a moment, breathless.

'He must have gone down through the secret passage,' said Lowe, and he made for the ivy-covered wall that screened the entrance. Pushing aside the thick growth, he felt his way down the steps, the others close at his heels. As they neared the bottom, there came a faint sound from somewhere in front: the sound of stumbling footsteps.

'You're right,' breathed White, his lips close to his employer's ear. 'He's down here.'

Without replying, Lowe hurried forward. It was difficult going in the dark, for he dare not use his torch in case the man they were after was armed, and twice he stumbled and almost fell as his feet caught on the uneven floor. But in spite of the darkness and the comparative slowness of their movements, they were gaining on their quarry, for now they could hear the sharp, irregular breathing of the man.

They were nearing the midway opening where the roof had fallen in when fate suddenly took a hand in their favour. There came a sudden muffled cry from the man in front, followed by a heavy thud. In his haste, their quarry had tripped and fallen. Before he could recover himself and scramble to his feet, Lowe was on him. He fought desperately, but the dramatist succeeded in getting a grip on his wrists and, with a sudden twist, jerked him round and brought his arms up sharply behind his back.

'Quick!' he panted to White and Shadgold. 'Get hold of him! I'm going to give you a surprise.'

They hauled the struggling fugitive to his feet and propped him against the wall. He was still trying vainly to free himself from their grip when Lowe pulled his torch from his pocket and, pressing the button, shone the light full on him. And then they all three uttered a simultaneous gasp of surprise.

The man they were holding was Dr. McGuire!

23

Dr. McGuire Tells the Truth

The lids of Dr. McGuire's small eyes blinked rapidly in the light of the torch, and he looked at Trevor Lowe with a malignant expression. 'This is the second time you have assaulted me, Mr. Lowe,' he snarled viciously.

'And on each occasion it's been entirely your own fault,' retorted the dramatist coolly. 'Perhaps you're prepared to offer an explanation for your presence here at this hour in the morning?'

The other maintained a sullen silence.

'Come now,' went on Lowe after he had waited in vain for the doctor to speak. 'I should advise you, unless you want a considerable amount of unpleasantness, to tell us the truth.'

'I suppose, under the circumstances, I'd better tell you,' the doctor grunted ungraciously, 'though I must say it goes against the grain. I strongly object to having my private business pried into. If I tell you the truth, will you give me your word that you'll keep the matter to yourself?'

'It's impossible for me to promise that,' Lowe said. 'I'll go as far as this, however — if the explanation for your presence in this passage has no connection with the business on which I'm engaged, and you can prove that to my satisfaction, then I'll do my best to respect your confidence.'

'It has a connection,' said Dr. McGuire, 'but not in the way you imagine.' He frowned and thought for a moment. 'I, too, am interested in the events that have been occurring around Monk's Lodge, but from a different angle to any of you. I am a poor man, Mr. Lowe. I hate to tell you this, because as I said before, I dislike discussing my private affairs with anybody. But you've got me cornered, and needs must when the devil drives.

'What little capital I had, I spent in buying this practice; and when I took possession, it would have been difficult for me to lay my hands on five pounds. Perhaps I'm the wrong sort of man for the people round these parts. I haven't the proper oily bedside manner, and I can't discuss with them the shortcomings of their friends and relations, or pretend to take an interest in their private affairs which I don't feel. Perhaps, on the other hand, they resent the advent of a stranger — I believe my predecessor was here for nearly twenty-five years.

'Something had to be done to augment the exchequer. I receive a small fee, it's true, for acting as divisional surgeon to the district, but it's far from enough; and some weeks ago, in order to make both ends meet, I utilised my spare time by writing one or two short articles for the press. I got some of them accepted, and then it occurred to me that I might still further add to my slender resources by becoming the special correspondent for this district.

'I wrote to the editor making my suggestion, and received a reply agreeing to it. I was to supply any news of interest that happened in King's Hayling and the surrounding neighbourhood. The payment was very small, but the job was not a particularly difficult one. I sent up three or four small paragraphs containing news of general interest, and then came the murder of Ogden and Friar's Vale, and Monk's Lodge at once became notorious. The editor of my paper, which is a fairly well-known London journal, wrote me to say that he was sending down a reporter to cover the business, and would I give him all the help I could. It struck me that if I could get permission, I could make a decent sum of money by handling the matter entirely myself. I got on the phone to the editor and told him my proposition. I said that I was in a better position to find out things than a stranger would be, as people were more likely to talk to me than they would be to someone they didn't know. He was a bit dubious at first, but eventually I talked him round, and he agreed, that so long as I could keep him supplied with good copy and the latest developments, I could carry on off my own bat.

'Now this was all right as far as it went, but there was a snag. As the divisional surgeon for the district, I had to keep my connection with the press a secret. Nor, if it had come out, would it have done me any good so far as my reputation as a doctor was concerned. But it did supply me with a certain amount of money — and that, in my financial state, was a tremendous consideration.

'Up to now I've been able to satisfy the editor's needs; and then, when things got slack and I had nothing to send through, it suddenly occurred to me some good copy might be got out of this passage. I'd already notified the paper of its discovery, and I thought I could follow that up with a short descriptive article which would keep the interest alive until something more sensational came along.

'There you are — that's the explanation, and I hope you're satisfied!'

'I suppose you have no objection to us confirming this?' said Lowe. 'I don't doubt your word, but —'

'Whether I've any objection or not wouldn't make much difference, would it?' snapped McGuire. 'The editor's name is Whyles, and the paper's the *Megaphone.* I don't suppose it's necessary for me to give you the address, as you know that, of course.'

Lowe nodded.

'Then I may as well be going,' said the doctor. 'Good night!' He pulled a torch from his pocket, switched it on and, brushing roughly past Shadgold, began to make his way along the passage towards the exit.

They watched the wavering beam of light until it disappeared round a bend, and then Shadgold gave a grunt of disgust. 'Well, we've lost the other fellow,' he said, 'and we're not likely to find him now. Might as well get back to the cottage.' He began to move slowly in the direction whence they had come. 'What do you suggest we do about this man Luckman?' he added. 'Arrest him straight away?'

'It depends,' said the dramatist. 'I'll answer that when I've had a look at that door in the cottage.'

He lapsed into silence, and did not speak again until they were crossing the lawn towards the still-open dining room window.

'You slip in,' he said to White, 'and open the front door for us.'

His secretary obeyed, and by the time they had reached the little porch the door was open. Lowe made straight for the dining room and, having lighted the lamp, carried it over to the door on which the man in the long coat had spent so many laborious hours.

He gave a grunt of disappointment as he examined the paintless patch. 'Not a trace left,' he said, turning to Shadgold. 'No, I don't think we shall arrest Luckman just yet. I'm rather anxious that the job should be completed properly, and if we arrest him now we can say goodbye to the diamonds. If I know anything about him, he'll keep his mouth shut and refuse to tell us where they are.'

'It's rather risky,' said Shadgold. 'He may get away altogether.'

'I don't think so,' replied the dramatist. 'You put those men on to watch the place as I suggested, didn't you?'

The inspector nodded.

'Well, what do we do now?' said White, yawning. 'Sleep?'

'You can if you like,' replied the dramatist, 'but I've got another job to do.'

'What's that?' demanded the Scotland

Yard man.

'I want to make a close examination of that secret passage,' Lowe said. 'I've got an idea that somewhere in there we shall find the last remaining piece of the puzzle.'

'What piece?' asked White, frowning.

'The missing piece,' answered Trevor Lowe. 'The piece that hasn't come to light yet — the other body!'

24

The Secret of the Passage

The sun was up, stretching golden fingers across the gloom of the wood, when Trevor Lowe and Shadgold, accompanied by White, whose desire for sleep had suddenly evaporated at the prospect of doing something, returned to the entrance of the underground passage by the ruins of the old monastery. The dark ivy-covered slit looked anything but inviting. As a contrast to the beauty of the morning, the fresh sweet-smelling breeze, and the twittering of the birds, it looked a decidedly unpleasant place.

Lowe parted the dense greenery and, switching on his electric torch, made his way down the stone stairs into the blackness below.

'How do you propose to start the search?' said Shadgold. 'Have you decided on any particular spot, or do we just make a general examination of the whole place?'

'A general examination of the whole place,' said the dramatist. 'We'll begin with this end and work our way gradually towards the exit by the river, and we had better each take a part of the tunnel and work that way. You've both got torches. I suggest that you and White take the left- and right-hand walls respectively, and I'll take the floor.'

'And what exactly are we looking for?' asked the Scotland Yard man.

'Any trace of a place where a body might be hidden,' replied Lowe. 'Any signs of a fairly fresh disturbance of the earth or brickwork.'

They made their way into the mouth of the tunnel and began the examination, moving slowly forward and subjecting the walls, roof and flooring to the most scrupulous inspection. They examined every inch of the floor and the rough-hewn walls, but there was nowhere a hiding-place could have been contrived even to secrete a mouse, and they went on into the short passage which led to the place where the roof had fallen in. There was nothing here, either. The walls, though falling away in places, had been untouched since the time the place was built; the flooring of irregular slabs was thickly covered with grime and dust; and although there were clear traces of footprints, there was nothing else.

They arrived at the great heap of fallen rubble that marked the place where the roof had collapsed without any discovery at all, and here they paused while Lowe lit a cigarette.

'Begins to look as though we're on a wild goose chase,' said Shadgold.

The dramatist nodded his agreement. 'As I said before,' he remarked, 'it was only a possibility. At the same time, there's still the other side of the passage. We may find what we're looking for there.'

But he proved to be wrong, for they reached the screened exit by the river without any better result than they had had before.

'There's just one place we haven't looked,' said the dramatist. 'That heap of rubbish under the opening in the wood. We might as well make certain about that!'

He turned and led the way back quickly

to the huge mass of fallen debris.

'It's difficult to tell whether this has been disturbed recently or not,' he said, standing and looking at it. 'I'm afraid the only thing we can do in this case is set to work and clear it away.'

The burly inspector eyed the heap dubiously. 'That's not going to be easy,' he grunted.

'It shouldn't take very long,' said Lowe. He turned to White. 'Cut along back to the cottage and see if you can find a couple of spades.'

White nodded and disappeared into the darkness of the passage. Seating themselves on the side of the mound, Lowe and Shadgold waited as patiently as possible for his return.

It was half an hour before the secretary came back, armed with two rather worn spades and an ancient gardening fork. 'Here you are,' he said with a grin. 'That's the entire contents of the tool-shed.'

Trevor Lowe took off his coat and selected a spade, Shadgold and White following suit, and they set to work to clear the rubbish heap. It was by no means easy work, and at the expiration of half an hour they had made little headway. It was not as if the pile consisted merely of fallen earth; time and again they had to stop and remove with their hands great pieces of cemented brickwork and the half-rotten branches of trees.

They had been working for nearly three hours when suddenly the dramatist uttered a sharp exclamation and dropped his spade. 'Come here!' he called, and Shadgold and White hurried to his side. He had just pulled away a curved piece of the fallen roof, and protruding from the cavity from which this had come was a foot!

'Look at that,' said Lowe grimly. 'We haven't had our trouble for nothing, after all!'

Shadgold whistled softly. 'We'd better get that uncovered as quickly as possible,' he said, and Lowe nodded. It took them some time, but eventually they succeeded in extricating the dead man from the litter under which he had been buried.

It required no medical knowledge to see that he had been dead for some time, and the blow that had crashed in the back of his skull and caused his death only served to add to his unpleasant appearance. He must have been lying there buried in that heap of debris for nearly a month! His clothes were rotting and dropping to pieces, and the flesh of the face and hands were discoloured and mottled.

Stifling his natural repugnance, Lowe bent over the body and searched the pockets. They had evidently been rifled by the man who had killed him, for he found nothing.

'Identification is not going to be so easy,' he said as he straightened up. 'It's doubtful if anybody would be able to recognise him from this appearance. The passage of time since he was killed hasn't helped matters there.'

'We know who he is, anyway,' said Shadgold.

'Yes, but what we've got to do is to convince a jury,' Lowe said. 'There may be some marks on his clothes, but at the present moment I don't think we should touch them — anyway, not until after the medical examination.'

'That's going to be difficult,' muttered

Shadgold. 'Who are you going to get — McGuire?'

'No.' Lowe shook his head. 'We don't want the discovery of the body to become public property yet, otherwise we shall scare our man away. Once he hears that we've found this, he'll realise the game's up. We'd better get a doctor from one of the outlying districts.'

'What are we going to do with the body in the meanwhile?' asked Shadgold. 'We can't very well leave it here. He knows about this secret passage, and if anything should bring him round this way he'll find it and guess that we've discovered it!'

'We shall have to take it back to Monk's Lodge,' said Lowe, 'and replace this rubbish on its original pile.'

The Scotland Yard man scratched his bullet head and made a dubious grimace. 'It's going to be a difficult job,' he said.

'I know,' replied Lowe, 'but it's got to be done. The best thing we can do is improvise some kind of stretcher.' He thought for a moment. 'Listen, White,' he went on presently, 'go along to the vault and bring back that monk's robe. With the help of that and these spades, I think we may be able to fix up what we want.'

His secretary hurried away, and during his absence Lowe and the inspector filled in the time by transferring a good portion of the rubble they had removed back to the main heap. They had almost completed this when White came back with the coarse black garment over one arm.

Lowe spread it out on the ground, and after a little trouble succeeded in manufacturing a rough stretcher. They lifted the body onto this carefully; and while White went ahead with the torch to light the way, Lowe and Shadgold followed with their grim burden between them. From here to the cottage was only a short distance, and a quarter of an hour later the remains of the dead man had been deposited carefully in one of the bedrooms.

'And now,' said the dramatist as he locked the door and followed Shadgold and White down the stairs, 'I think we might have something to eat before we pay a visit to Friar's Vale.'

'Friar's Vale?' The Scotland Yard man raised his eyebrows.

'We're going to call on Mr. Wyse,' replied Lowe. 'I think the time has come when a heart-to-heart talk with that gentleman seems rather necessary!'

25

The Barn

Mr. Wyse moved his head uneasily and became aware of a dull, throbbing ache in his skull. He made a feeble attempt to raise his hand in order to ease this pounding hammer that was beating at his temples. But his hand and arm were immovable.

He opened his eyes slowly, wincing at the sharp, stabbing pain the action caused. He saw a void of greyish blackness, but presently this grew clearer, and he discovered that he was staring at a slanting roof supported by heavy beams which showed faintly in a dim illumination. He was lying on his back on a heap of something soft, and the reason for the immovability of his hands and arms, he found after a little experimenting, was because they had been securely bound behind his back with thick cord.

Ignoring the pain it caused him, he turned his head sideways in order to see more of his surroundings. The place was littered with dirty straw, broken bits of planking, and empty packing-cases. The dim light came from a piece of candle that was stuck on the top of one of these, and which scarcely did more than render the darkness in the corners more intense. The floor, what little he could see of it, was of mud, and the whole place smelt indescribably musty; a peculiar odour of rottenness which presently he decided was the smell of decaying grain. A heap of half-filled sacks in one corner, through the rotting fabric of which the contents had streamed out onto the floor, bore out this supposition. The place was obviously a barn of some sort, and clearly had not been used for the purpose for which it had been built for some considerable time.

As his brain grew clearer, memory came flooding back. He remembered leaving his cottage and setting off down the road in the direction of the lane that led to Monk's Lodge. It had been his intention to visit the tenantless cottage and to further continue his search for the clue which he sought.

He remembered the dim outline of the

car with its lights out which he had seen drawn up near the end of the lane, and there memory failed him, for he had only the vaguest recollection of what had happened after that. He had paused to look at the car curiously, wondering why it should be waiting at that particular spot. Then something had rushed at him out of the darkness of the night, and before he had had time to defend himself a heavy weight crashed down on his head and he knew no more. A blank interval elapsed between that time and the time when he had slowly recovered his senses, to find himself lying trussed up in this disused and dilapidated barn.

He had no illusions as to who his attacker had been. It was, of course, the man Murdock. This was the third attempt. There had been the burglary at the cottage and the shots in the lane, both of which had proved unsuccessful. This time they had apparently succeeded in their object — or, rather, Murdock had; for Blane, his companion, no longer existed.

Well, Murdock would be disappointed. He would get nothing. He had gone to a great deal of trouble, and his gain would be precisely nil.

His head still throbbed painfully, but his first feeling of giddiness and nausea was rapidly wearing off. He wondered vaguely what the time was, and how long he had been unconscious, and where his assailant and captor had gone to.

It was raining outside; he could hear the steady swish of it and the drip, drip, where it was coming in through the leaky roof. He lay for a long time listening to the monotonous sound, and then, after a lapse of what he judged roughly to be about half an hour, there mingled with the noise of the rain the squelch of approaching footsteps. They drew nearer and nearer. Then there came the rattle of a padlock, the door was thrown open, and a man in a gripping mackintosh entered. He took off his sodden cap and wrung out the water, and the bound man on the floor caught sight of the white face and little black beard, and knew that his conjectures had not been wrong. It was Murdock!

The man flung the limp rag of his cap down on the packing-case beside the candle, and then, coming over, stared down at his captive. 'So you've recovered your senses, have you?' he said harshly. 'Good! Now we can get down to business!'

Wyse regarded him steadily, but made no reply.

'You know why I've brought you here,' Murdock continued, 'so there's no need for me to explain that. The question is, are you going to be sensible and tell me what I want to know at once, or are you going to put me to a lot of trouble and make me drag the information out of you?'

'I have no information to give you,' said Wyse quietly.

'Oh you haven't, eh?' snarled the bearded man. 'We'll see about that. It's no good trying to pull that stuff on me, Luckman. I want those diamonds and I'm going to have them!'

'You're making a great mistake,' said the other.

'It's no good trying that bluff on me. I'll admit your make-up's pretty good, but you always were clever at disguises. Now then, are you going to tell me where those diamonds are?'

'No, for the simple reason I have no more idea than you have,' retorted the bound man.

'So that's the line you're going to take, is it?' Murdock hissed menacingly. 'Well, you can't say that I haven't warned you. I'm going to make you speak if I have to tear you to pieces! Now then, I'll give you one more chance — where are those diamonds?'

'I tell you you've made a mistake,' said Wyse. 'You think I'm Luckman, but I'm not.'

'Of course you're not,' sneered the bearded man. 'You never committed the robbery in Hatton Garden, did you? You never did in the watchman? You never went to Broadmoor? You never had two pals called Murdock and Blane, whom you tried to double-cross? Oh, no, of course not! I've made a mistake — you're the Archbishop of Canterbury — I don't think!' He dropped his bantering tone suddenly. 'You fool — you bloody fool! Do you think you can get away with that with me? I've been watching you ever since you came to Friar's Vale, and I'll stake my life you're Luckman!'

'Then you would lose it,' said Wyse

292

calmly. 'Haven't you got eyes, man? Do I look like Joseph Luckman?'

'How do I know?' snapped Murdock. 'I never saw Luckman as he really looked. He was always disguised — you know that. What's the good of denying that you're Luckman?'

'Because it's the truth,' said the other.

'You can go on telling me that until you're blue in the face,' grated Murdock, 'but I shan't believe you! I tell you, I've been watching you for nearly a month, so it's no good trying to kid me on those lines. Now look here, I'll give you just half an hour to make up your mind. If at the expiration of that time you still decide to be stubborn, so much the worse for you!'

He walked over to the packing-case, picked up his cap and pulled it down low over his eyes. Crossing to the door, he paused with it half-open in his hand. 'If you take my advice, you will be sensible when I come back, for I shall bring with me a means of persuading you.'

He disappeared into the darkness outside, closing the door behind him, and the bound man heard the rattle of a key in the padlock. Murdock's footsteps faded to silence and Wyse was left alone with his thoughts, which were decidedly unpleasant ones.

★   ★   ★

'Look here,' said Jack Denton, throwing down his book, 'I'm sick of this! It's too bad of Lowe to leave us cooped up in this rotten hotel while all the excitement's going on.'

Tony Frost looked across at his friend and grinned. 'Yes, it's pretty rough luck,' he admitted. 'But Lowe was most emphatic, you know. He told us to stop here and not to show ourselves on any account until we heard from him. It's pretty boring, I know, but I'm afraid it's got to be done.'

Trevor Lowe had given them no explanation for his sudden desire to vacate the cottage at Monk's Lodge, and they had both been firmly under the impression that when he had said that he was leaving for London he was speaking the truth. It was not until they were actually in the train that the dramatist had exploded his bombshell and informed them that he had no intention of travelling further than the next stop, which was at Sunnington, a few miles beyond King's Hayling, where the train stopped to pick up the mail.

They had lunched at Sunnington and in the early afternoon had walked back to King's Hayling, where Lowe had ensconced them in the Railway Hotel and left them with strict instructions to stop there until he came back.

Tony was fairly content to adhere to these instructions; but Jack, who had planned a visit to Ursula Wyse, found the slow passage of time irksome. He saw no reason why they should be planted here like left luggage, without any explanation as to the why or wherefore, but he stuck it as best he could until with the approach of dusk his patience became exhausted.

'I can't stop here mooning about any longer,' he said irritably. 'I'm going out for a walk. It can't possibly do any harm.'

'You know what Lowe said,' began Tony.

'Never mind what Lowe said,' Jack snapped. 'I don't suppose he meant literally that we aren't to show our noses outside the front door! Besides, it's too dark now for anybody to recognise me. Nobody knows me round this place.'

'Well, you can please yourself, old man,' said Tony. 'Personally, I'm going to stop here. Lowe said distinctly —'

'You keep on repeating that like a parrot!' broke in Jack. 'I'm going to use my own discretion.'

Tony shrugged. 'Where are you going?'

Jack's face assumed an expression of elaborate casualness. 'Oh, just round about,' he murmured vaguely. 'I shan't be long.' He picked up his hat and crossed to the door.

'I don't think you ought to go, you know,' said Tony indecisively as his fingers turned the handle.

* * *

'Oh, nonsense!' said Jack over his shoulder. He closed the door behind him and made his way down the stairs.

There was nobody in the small vestibule of the hotel as he passed outside, except the woman behind the reception-desk, and she never even glanced up. He paused for a moment or two, glancing from left to right.

Although he had been deliberately vague regarding his intentions to Tony, he had definitely decided that his walk was to be far from an aimless stroll. The irresistible desire to see Ursula was not to be put aside.

It was a fairly long walk to Friar's Vale, and Jack scarcely realised that it would take so much time. It had been a little after half-past nine when he had left the hotel, and the cracked bell of Friar's Vale's ancient church was striking eleven as he hove in sight of the Wyses' cottage. There were lights in the hall and sitting-room; he could see them faintly through the trees when he was still some considerable distance away. Now, for the first time, doubt began to creep into his mind. The hour was late. What reasonable excuse could he offer for calling?

He went slowly by, and a few yards down the road turned and retraced his steps. He could think of nothing that sounded at all convincing. That there was really no need for any excuse at all never crossed his mind. It would have been the most natural thing in the world for him to have dropped in casually and inquired after Mr. Wyse's health, or even just said that he happened to be passing and saw the light. But Jack possessed a totally exaggerated idea that unless he was provided with a cast-iron reason, both Wyse and Ursula would immediately guess the real object of his visit.

He passed the gate twice, trying to summon up sufficient courage to enter and knock at the inviting front door; and then, as he stopped several yards away, the door of the cottage opened, and Mr. Wyse himself came out. He was clearly visible in the fan-shaped wedge of light that streamed down the little path, and as he reached the gate he turned and waved his hand before hurrying down the road in the direction of the lane that led to Monk's Lodge. Evidently the person he had waved to was Ursula, thought Jack, and here in the unexpected appearance of the old man was the excuse he wanted. If he could overtake Wyse and accompany him on his walk, it was ten chances to one that he would be invited back to the cottage.

He set off in Wyse's wake, but had scarcely gone half a dozen yards before it became clearly evident that this was no ordinary constitutional that the other was taking. He was moving rapidly, and there was purpose in his every stride. Jack altered his mind, and instead of trying to catch up with him, slowed his pace so that he remained about fifty yards behind.

Where was the old man going in such a hurry, and at such an hour?

The answer seemed fairly obvious; for, apart from the lane that led up to the cottage at Monk's Lodge, the road went nowhere except out into the open country. There was no other house, so far as Jack knew, within a distance of seven miles, and it was thoroughly unlikely that Wyse would be setting out after eleven o'clock at night to call upon a neighbour.

No, the only possible place he could be making for was Monk's Lodge, and it struck Jack that this was distinctly odd. Wyse must have heard that they had vacated the place. Lowe had been very particular to have that fact spread around the village.

What in the world, then, was he going there for?

Jack remembered the incident of the sponge and the water. Was there to be another wall-washing expedition? He was determined to find out. All thought of making his presence known to Wyse had evaporated. Keeping close to the hedge at the side of the road, so that it would be difficult for the other to see him if he looked round, Jack followed.

The night was very dark, for the storm-clouds which later were to descend in a torrential downpour were piling up across the sky, and he had considerable difficulty in keeping the other in sight. Near the entrance to the lane he lost him altogether in the dense blackness caused by a clump of tall trees that edged the road at this spot. He could hear his footsteps, however, and suddenly the rapid walk slowed hesitantly, and then stopped altogether. Had Wyse discovered that he was being followed?

Then from somewhere ahead came a sharp cry — a cry that snapped off abruptly in the middle, like the sudden stoppage of a gramophone in the midst of a note.

Jack remembered the attack on the old man in the lane previously, and began to run forward. He had covered several yards when close at hand in front of him he heard the whirring of a self-starter, followed by the rhythmic throb-throb of a car engine. The sound rose in a rapid crescendo to a roar, and a dark black blot swung out from the side of the road and began to move away.

It was a car without lights; and even as Jack caught a momentary glimpse of it, the driver changed from first to second gear and then to top speed, and the sound of the engine faded in the distance.

Jack paused by the mouth of the lane, panting. Then, striking a match, he looked about him in the feeble glimmer, half-fearful of what he would find. But he found nothing. There was no sign of Mr. Wyse, well or injured. He had disappeared with the car, and Jack was pretty certain that he had not gone willingly!

26

Just in Time!

To the bound man lying helpless on the heap of rotten sacking, an eternity seemed to pass before he heard the returning footsteps of his captor.

'Well,' Murdock said as he shut the door behind him, 'have you thought better of your confounded stubbornness?'

'You're asking me to do an impossibility,' Wyse replied. 'I cannot tell you what you want to know, for the simple reason that I don't know myself.'

'Still adamant, are you?' hissed the other. 'All right — we'll see if this will loosen your tongue.' He took a bottle from his coat-pocket. 'This bottle contains petrol, and I'm going to let it drop into your eyes until you decide to tell me what I want to know. I should think that would be somewhere after the third drop, for I understand that the raw spirit burns rather badly.'

He saw the expression of the other's face and laughed harshly. 'I see that you have a vivid imagination,' he said. 'Now, before I begin the — er — operation, I'll give you one more chance. Where have you hidden those diamonds?'

'I've told you repeatedly that you're making a mistake,' said Wyse. 'I am not Luckman, and I do not know where the diamonds are hidden.'

'Very well, then,' said Murdock furiously, 'you've only yourself to blame, and you can take the consequences.'

He bent down and, jerking the cork from the bottle, tilted it above Mr. Wyse's upturned face. It was half-full of a colourless liquid, and the helpless man watched this as it slowly crept up the side of the bottle towards the neck. Slowly, very slowly, Murdock twisted it, apparently taking a fiendish delight in prolonging the suspense.

The petrol reached the shoulder of the bottle and entered the narrow neck. A little bead gathered on the lip, and Mr. Wyse involuntarily closed his eyes.

'Will you tell me?' hissed Murdock below his breath — and at that moment the door crashed open behind him.

With an oath, he sprang to his feet and swung round, his hand flying to the pocket of his coat. But before he could draw the weapon he was searching for, the newcomer had launched himself upon him. Borne backwards by the force of the other's rush, Murdock fell heavily, the petrol-bottle spilling as it struck the floor.

The force of the impact drove the breath from his body, and he struggled frantically to free himself from the hands that were gripping his throat. He lashed out viciously with his foot, but his attacker, with a twist, dodged the kick. Murdock clawed at his wrists, but he could not break that grip, and suddenly adopting a new tactic, he swung round his right in a short-arm jab at the other's chin. The blow connected with a thud, and the hold on his throat relaxed.

It was only for a moment, but in that moment Murdock succeeded in wrenching himself free. He struggled to his knees, but before he could regain his feet his opponent had recovered, and was on him. They rolled over and over, fighting desperately, and narrowly missed overturning the packing-case with the candle.

Murdock tried hard to reach the gun in his pocket, but he never got a chance. They brought up with a crash against the wall, and that was the end of things so far as Murdock was concerned, for his head came in violent contact with a heavy upright beam, and amidst a fountain of orange flame his senses left him.

Breathless and dishevelled, Jack Denton rose to his feet and tenderly caressed his jaw. 'By Jove, that was hot while it lasted!' he exclaimed, and crossed over to the bound figure.

A few slashes with his penknife severed the cords, and he helped the older man to his feet. It was some time before Wyse could regain the use of his limbs, for the impeded circulation had rendered them numb and practically useless. But presently, after much rubbing, he succeeded in restoring them to something like normal.

'I think I arrived just in time,' remarked Jack when he had almost recovered.

'I think you did,' agreed Mr. Wyse.

Lowe and Shadgold left White behind at the cottage and set off for Friar's Vale. Dawn had already broken as they strode down the lane. They were nearing a turning when two figures came into view about two hundred yards further on. They recognised them simultaneously.

'Good God! Wyse and Denton!' exclaimed the dramatist in astonishment, and he hurried forward to meet the newcomers.

In the bright light of the sun they both looked like tramps. Mr. Wyse's clothes were shapeless and stained. One side of his grey head was dark with dried blood, which had run in streaks down his white collar and splashed onto his shirt. His shoes were covered in mud, and he looked thoroughly ill and exhausted. Jack Denton was nearly as bad. He looked like the more respectable species of scarecrow. His jacket was split across the back, there were rents in his trousers, and one of his eyes was completely closed and rapidly assuming a beautiful shade of purple. He grinned one-sidedly as Lowe and Shadgold came up to them.

'What on earth are you doing here, Denton?' asked the dramatist.

'Seeing Mr. Wyse home,' replied Jack. 'We've had a most exciting night.' He briefly explained what had happened. 'I bound up the bearded fellow,' he went on, 'before he had recovered consciousness, and we left him in the barn — you'll find him there.'

'Where is the place?' asked Shadgold.

'About ten miles further along this road,' replied Jack, 'on the other side of a ploughed field. That's why we've been so long getting back. We started off in the other fellow's car, which, by the way —' He looked at Lowe. '—is the one that brought us from King's Hayling the day you arrived, but the beastly thing broke down before we had gone more than half a mile — some water had got into the magneto. We sat in it for a long time hoping that somebody would pass from whom we could beg a lift, but nobody did. Finally we decided the only way to get here was to walk, so we started, and here we are. The thing I want most is some breakfast.'

'What about Murdock?' said the Scotland Yard man, looking at Lowe. 'Oughtn't we to go and secure him right away?'

'He's safe enough,' broke in Jack. 'He's trussed up like a chicken and can scarcely move an eyelid.'

'I think we might as well leave him until later on,' said Lowe. 'There are one or two rather urgent questions that I would like to ask Mr.—er — er —Wyse!'

The grey-haired man smiled. 'I've no doubt there are,' he said dryly, 'and if you'll wait until I've had something in the nature of breakfast, I shall be prepared to answer them.'

'Right, that's a bargain,' said Trevor Lowe, and they all four set off for the cottage.

27

Sydney Garth Explains

'Now,' said Mr. Wyse nearly an hour and a half later, as he stretched himself in an easy chair, 'you can ask me anything you like.'

The remains of the breakfast that Ursula had hastily prepared still stood on the little table in the sitting-room, and although Lowe and Shadgold themselves had not eaten anything, they had been glad of the coffee their host had pressed upon them.

'All I want to ask you,' said Lowe, setting down his empty cup, 'is just how you're connected with this affair. To start with, who are you? Unfortunately, your present name of Wyse does not coincide with the initials 'S.G.' that mark your linen.'

The grey-haired man's eyes twinkled. 'So you noticed those, Mr. Lowe, did you?' he said with a smile. 'Now when did you have a chance to see them?'

'That night you were attacked in the

lane,' replied Lowe. 'I loosened your collar, and —'

'That's bad, very bad.' Mr. Wyse shook his head. 'I really must remember in future to pay more attention to details. However, you're quite right, Mr. Lowe. My name is not Wyse. My real name is Sydney Garth, and to a lesser degree, I follow the same profession as your friend.'

'You mean you're a detective?' Lowe asked, a little gleam of understanding coming into his eyes.

'Yes,' Garth answered. 'Though I call myself a private inquiry agent. I have an office in the city, and have for years undertaken all kinds of confidential matters. You've probably heard of Thoroughgood & Co.'

'I have,' broke in Shadgold. 'They're a very well-known firm of inquiry agents, and unlike most of the species, possess a very enviable reputation.'

'Thank you!' Mr. Garth inclined his head. 'Well, I am Thoroughgood, and my daughter is the 'Co'.' He looked across at Ursula, who was seated on the sofa beside Jack. 'We, of course, employ several other people in the firm, but the more important business we deal with ourselves.'

'And how do you come to be mixed up in this particular business?' inquired Lowe.

'The answer to that is quite simple,' replied Garth. 'I am employed by the Hatton Garden Diamond firm, whom Luckman robbed.'

'I see,' said the dramatist softly.

'They were never very sure,' continued Garth, 'that those diamonds had ever been thrown into the Thames at all, and when the search by the police failed to find them they approached me. From the outset I considered that it was rather a hopeless task, but I have a certain amount of pride, and I thought it would be a distinct feather in the cap of Thoroughgood & Co. if we succeeded where the police had failed. I had nothing at all to go on — not the slightest vestige of a clue; but I remembered that Luckman had been arrested in a cheap little lodging-house, and thinking the matter over, it struck me that this place could hardly be his permanent abode.

'I had attended the trial, and studied him carefully. He was not the type of man to live habitually in such surroundings as those in which he had been found. Following this train of thought, I came to the conclusion that he must have had some other headquarters hitherto unsuspected and unknown, and that if the diamonds were not at the bottom of the Thames, then the most likely place they would be was at this unknown retreat.

'Having come to this conclusion,' he went on, 'the next step was to find this place of Luckman's — if it existed. This was by no means an easy task, and entailed an enormous amount of spade work. I put three of my best men specially on the job, and had inquiries instituted all over the country. We worked to a method. Taking London as a centre, we worked in ever-widening circles, my men instituting inquiries with all the estate agents, armed with a photograph of Luckman. We obtained no result from our diligence until we reached Dryseley, and the photograph was recognised by Mr. Ogden as that of a man who had bought a cottage called Monk's Lodge.

'To cut a long story short, we eventually established beyond any reasonable doubt that this was the place we had been looking for, and we established it without letting Ogden know the real reason for our interest. All this, of course, took considerable time, and the day following my man's report I heard that Luckman had succeeded in escaping from Broadmoor. I decided that if my conjectures had been correct, and that the diamonds were hidden in or near Monk's Lodge, that would be the place he'd make for.

'In company with my daughter, who has worked with me on most of my more important cases, I came to King's Hayling, and in the name of Wyse rented this cottage. Monk's Lodge, I discovered, was temporarily occupied by two young men who had taken it for the duration of their holidays, and I wondered how this would affect Luckman's plan, if any. He'd already been free for over three weeks. I got my information from the newspapers, and I learned that they'd been instructed by the police to suppress the news of his escape for a time. For all I knew, he might have succeeded in securing the diamonds in the interim.

'Inquiries in the village elicited the fact

that some people called Cheply had been tenants of the cottage prior to its being taken by Mr. Frost and Mr. Denton, but they had left for America, and the cottage had been empty for some time. I reasoned that there would have been ample time for Luckman to have come, got what he wanted, and gone. I decided, however, to stay where I was for a few days and await developments. And I'm very glad I did, for almost immediately came the disappearance of Ogden, followed by the discovery of his body in the lumber-room of Monk's Lodge. That settled any doubt in my mind as to whether Luckman had been successful, and it also put to rest once and for all any idea that I was on a wild-goose chase.

'The diamonds had never been thrown into the Thames. There was some close connection between them and Monk's Lodge, and I was determined to find it out, and if possible recover the stones for my clients. If any further confirmation was needed, I got it on the night this house was burgled. The two men who did it evidently mistook me for Luckman, for they tried to force me to reveal where the diamonds were hidden. When I told them that I knew nothing about them, they chloroformed me with the intention, I firmly believe, of carrying me off to try further methods of persuasion, and were only prevented because they were disturbed by Ursula.

'I think that's about all. It was no doubt foolish of me not to take you and the police into my confidence, and let you know who I was and what I was actually doing here; but I'd worked for years on this matter, and I didn't want anybody else to step in at the last moment and reap the reward of my labours. I gave Ursula implicit instructions that on no account was she to reveal who we were or what we were here for. You can call it what you like — pride, conceit, anything, but I was rather anxious to finish the job off under my own steam.'

He stopped and looked round inquiringly. 'Anything you'd like to ask?'

'I should like to know,' said Lowe, 'what gave you the idea that there might be a clue to the hiding-place of the stones behind the whitewash on the walls of the cottage.'

'That,' said Garth with a smile, 'I must admit was rather a long shot. When I came down here to take this cottage I got it through Ogden, and during my conversation with him I led the talk round to Monk's Lodge. I told him that I'd passed the place and thought how pretty it was. I asked him what it was like inside, one thing led to another, and he told me quite casually that it was in fairly good repair, but that if it had been left to him it would have been redecorated nearly a year previously. He said, however, that the owner had strictly prohibited any of the interior paintwork or walls being touched. I thought about this for a long time, wondering what Luckman's reason could have been, and came to the conclusion that possibly the wash on the walls concealed some kind of hiding-place. Hence my experiment!'

'I see,' said Lowe. 'Well, you nearly hit the truth, but not quite. There's one more question I should like to ask. What was it your daughter picked up from the flowerbed on the afternoon she paid her visit to Monk's Lodge?'

'One of my cufflinks,' replied Garth. 'Unfortunately it had my initials on it. I lost it one night when I was prowling round on a voyage of exploration. As a matter of fact I heard it drop, but I hadn't got time to look for it myself, because somebody was moving about inside the cottage and I had no desire to be discovered there. But I made a mental note of the spot and sent Ursula up, when I thought everybody was out, to retrieve it. And now —' He looked quizzically at Lowe. '—I think it's my turn to do the asking. Just how much have you discovered?'

'Now that I've heard your story,' said the dramatist, 'pretty nearly everything!'

'You've found the diamonds?' asked the grey-haired man eagerly.

'Not yet,' Lowe answered, 'but I have every reason to hope that I shall find them tonight!'

'Tonight!' echoed Garth. 'What's going to happen tonight?'

'Unless I'm very much mistaken,' said Lowe quietly, 'tonight will see the final act of the drama. If everything goes as I expect it to, I hope tonight to be able to introduce you to Mr. Joseph Luckman!'

28

Interlude

Jack Denton, with his mind in a whirl from the turn of events, and rather hazy as to how he had got there, found himself strolling along the shady banks of the River Loam with Ursula.

At the conclusion of Sydney Garth's story, Lowe and the others had taken their departure, but Jack had remained behind in the hope of getting a few minutes with Ursula, and so successful had he been that before he knew where he was, she had agreed to his suggestion of a walk, and the suggestion had been endorsed by her father. They set off idly with no particular destination in mind, and coming suddenly upon the little river, followed its winding course.

For the most part their walk had been in silence. Jack had something to say and was trying to think of the best way of saying it, and Ursula's mind was, apparently, miles away. It could not have been so very far, however, for suddenly she looked up at her companion.

'I haven't thanked you for last night,' she said. 'If it hadn't been for you —' She shivered. '—God knows what would have happened to Father.'

'I'm glad I was lucky enough to be there,' said Jack. 'It was, after all, sheer luck, you know.'

'I don't think you're being quite fair to yourself,' she said. 'Well, now that you know the truth, what do you think about it?'

'I've given up thinking.' He smiled ruefully. 'I must admit, however, that I'm surprised to find that you're a — well, a kind of a detective.'

'I'm a very good detective,' she said a little coldly.

'Oh, I mean the fact that you're a detective at all is — er — rather astonishing.'

'Why?'

'I don't know.' He was floundering badly, and inwardly cursed himself for having started the subject. It was so far away from the one he wished to talk about. 'It seems all wrong for a — a woman to be mixed up in things like — like crime.'

She laughed — a musical sound that Jack thought blended rather well with the ripple of the water. 'You're rather old-fashioned, aren't you?' she said.

'Perhaps in a way, I am,' he replied. 'But there are some things that don't seem to mix.'

'And women and detectives is one of them?' She smiled demurely, and he noticed that she had a delightful dimple at the corner of her mouth.

'I don't know why you should think that,' she went on. 'All those ideas of keeping women on a pedestal away from the ordinary happenings of life, unsullied and scared for fear a draught should blow on them, are all nonsense. And you can take it from me, Mr. Denton, that women don't like it. They like to be credited with having sufficient brains to do a job as well as a man.'

'I suppose there's something in that if you look at it that way,' he admitted.

'I do look at it that way,' she insisted. 'I've spent some very happy times helping

Father. You see, I took a very real interest in the work. After a while, he got to look upon me as a real partner, and discussed everything with me. It was really my suggestion that brought us down here.'

'And a very good suggestion, too,' said Jack heartily — so heartily that she flushed. 'You misunderstand me if you think I hold the theory that women should be wrapped up in cotton wool. I don't! But in your case, think of the danger you must have been exposed to.'

'I've been exposed to very little more danger than any woman who ordinarily earns her living in the city,' she replied calmly. 'There's always danger there from traffic accidents and things. My father took care that I was not exposed to any other danger. I never participated in the really rough work. Our assistants, who are mostly ex-detectives, do all that.'

'I suppose when you come to analyse it, it's all right,' said Jack. 'This will mean a lot to you and your father, won't it? I mean, if the diamonds are found.'

'It would have done — if *we'd* found them,' she answered. 'But if the police find them, it won't mean anything.'

He thought this over. 'You haven't any idea where they are, have you?' he asked.

'Not the slightest,' she replied. 'I did think at one time that they were hidden in Monk's Lodge. I suppose you don't know what Mr. Lowe has in his mind about tonight?'

'Nobody knows what's in Lowe's mind except himself,' said Jack. 'But if he says that he's going to introduce us to this fellow Luckman, I wouldn't mind betting that he will.'

They had reached a spot where the Loam narrowed and the bank inclined steeply beside them, and by tacit consent they halted and sat down on a projection of the bank.

'I should like to be there,' murmured Ursula. 'I wonder if they'd let me come, too.'

'You mustn't think of it for a moment.'

'Why not? I'd very much like to know who he is.'

'Whoever he is, he's a madman, and dangerous,' said Jack.

'There you go again.' She sighed.

'Trotting out the pedestal and the cotton wool box.'

'I'm not,' said Jack angrily. 'There's a difference between that and acting sensibly, and allowing you to come with us tonight to — wherever we're going — would be sheer idiocy.'

Ursula looked a little annoyed. She was not used to having her wishes vetoed in this decisive way. 'That is surely for my father to decide,' she said.

'I've no doubt that your father would agree with me,' Jack replied stiffly. 'However, as you say, it's entirely a matter for him.' He fumbled in his pocket for his cigarette case, found it and lighted a cigarette.

'Do your prejudices include women smoking, too?'

There was a suspicious quiver to the voice, and he turned quickly. Ursula was biting her lip to try and stop her laughter.

'I'm terribly sorry,' he said, and dragged out his case and held it out to her.

'Thank you,' she said, and took a cigarette. He snapped open his lighter and held it to the tip. 'You know,' she went on when the cigarette was alight, 'this is all rather silly.'

'It is, isn't it?' agreed Jack. 'After all, you must remember that you tried to do the same for me as I was doing for you.'

'What do you mean?' she asked.

'Don't you remember?' He chuckled. 'You tried to get me to leave Monk's Lodge — twice. You were trying to keep me out of danger then.'

The dimple that Jack had admired before appeared again in her cheek. 'How do you know it was for that reason?' she murmured demurely. 'How do you know it wasn't because I wanted Monk's Lodge empty so that Father and I could search for the diamonds?'

'I gave you the benefit of the doubt,' he replied. 'And I hope I was right.'

'You were. I really *was* anxious about you. I think we'd better be getting back now, don't you?' she said, rising.

'No, I don't!' snapped Jack, and all his vain efforts at a carefully rehearsed speech were cast to the winds. Without quite knowing how she got there, Ursula found herself in his arms. 'Ursula,' he whispered,

'I love you very dearly.'

She looked up at him, and that aggravating dimple deepened. 'Why on earth,' she replied calmly, 'didn't you say that before instead of talking nonsense?'

For a very good reason, Jack made no reply.

29

The Hiding-place

Trevor Lowe was very busy for the rest of that day, and it was not until dusk was approaching that they once more met in the sitting-room of Garth's cottage. This arrangement had been made in the morning, before Lowe and Shadgold had taken their leave. Jack had stayed to lunch, and also for tea, which in the circumstances was not surprising. The party on this occasion, however, was larger than it had been before, for two extra people were present, in the persons of Tony Frost and White.

'We do nothing at present,' said the dramatist in answer to a question from their grey-haired host, 'except wait. You will know what we're waiting for very soon.'

'Well, whatever it is, I hope that I'm going to be in it,' said Tony. 'I missed all the excitement last night. I wondered what the deuce had happened when Jack never came back.'

'You should get enough later on to make up for it,' said Lowe grimly. 'By the way —' He looked at Jack. '—how did you manage to find that barn and arrive in time to save our friend from Murdock's tender attentions?'

'More by luck than anything. I knew that something very serious had happened to Mr. Wyse — Mr. Garth — but the car was out of sight before I could do anything. However, I wasn't going to leave it at that, so I followed as fast as I could. I didn't know the road, but I kept a sharp lookout for any side turnings down which the car might have gone.

'There were only three, as it happened; two of which were too narrow to allow the passage of a car, and one which I wasn't quite certain about. I wasted a lot of time exploring this, as a matter of fact, before I found that it ended in a barred gate that was chained and padlocked, and pretty obviously hadn't been opened. It didn't look as though the car had come down that way, so I came back to the main road and walked on. There were no side turnings of any description after that one with the gate, but I should never have found any trace of the car if I hadn't happened to see a light flash for a moment on my left as I was passing a ploughed field.

'It was unlikely that any of the ordinary inhabitants would be wandering about a ploughed field at that hour, I thought. And then I saw the light of the torch glint on the metalwork of a car. I was soaked to the skin, for I had been all through the storm, but the sight of that car cheered me up no end.

'I hopped over the railings into the field and made my way towards the light. It was not a nice field, and that rain hadn't made it any better. However, eventually I saw that I was nearing a barn. It was still raining pretty heavily, but by this time I was impervious to water. I could see a faint trickle of light coming from a crack in one side of the barn, and creeping up to this I found that it was wide enough to allow me to see in.

'I had a look, and was just in time to see the bearded chap doing his stuff with the bottle, and then I took a hand in the game, and that's that!'

'And all the time you were enjoying yourself,' remarked Tony, 'I was wandering about that mouldy hotel, wondering what in the world had happened! Well, Lowe has promised that tonight will make up for it. All I hope is that we haven't got to wait much longer!'

'You haven't got to wait *any* longer,' said Lowe. 'Listen! That's what we've been waiting for!'

From outside came a low, clear whistle. With a word of apology, the dramatist crossed to the door and went out into the hall. There was a pause, and then they heard the low whispering of voices. Presently he came back.

'Come along,' he said. 'It's time we started.'

They followed him, collecting their hats from the hall stand as they passed. A man was standing outside in the darkness, and he saluted Inspector Shadgold as the latter crossed the threshold.

'Everything all right, Dickinson?' asked the Scotland Yard man.

'Yes, sir,' replied the plainclothes man.

'He left five minutes ago. Parrish is following him.'

'Good!' grunted Shadgold.

Trevor Lowe turned to the little party. 'I must ask you all to refrain from talking,' he said, 'and to move with as little noise as possible. Mr. Dickinson here will lead the way, and we'd better keep as close together as we can. All right, Dickinson.'

The plainclothes man turned and made his way down the little path to the gate. Tony noticed that he stooped forward slightly as he walked, keeping his eyes fixed on the ground, and, following his example, was surprised to see a thin, scattered trail of confetti that showed up dimly on the dark surface of the road.

'What are we going to — a wedding?' he asked Lowe, who was walking by his side.

'No,' the dramatist replied in a low voice. 'Parrish, who's following the man we're after, was told to leave that trail so that we should be able to tell which way he went. Otherwise it would've been impossible for us to follow him.'

They pursued the trail to the edge of a little thicket, where they met Parrish. Some hundred yards away was a dim figure with a light.

'Everything all right, Parrish?' murmured Lowe, his lips close to the man's ear.

'Yes, sir,' was the almost inaudible reply.

'Right!' The dramatist turned to White. 'Listen,' he said, and his whisper was so faint that Tony, who was little more than a yard away, could not hear a sound. 'We're going forward to close in on him. You stop here with the others and guard this point.'

He moved away into the darkness with Shadgold and the two plainclothes men. They faded away into the shadows, and their passing was as silent as a well-oiled machine.

Tony's eyes had become fairly well accustomed to the darkness by now, and in the reflected light of the torch he was able to make out what that dim figure ahead was doing. It was kneeling by the trunk of a massive tree, digging furiously with some small object that Tony guessed was a trowel.

Something must have warned the man ahead there by the tree that he was no longer alone, for suddenly he ceased his digging operations and sprang to his feet, standing motionless in an attitude that betokened intense listening. He twisted his head from side to side in little sharp, jerky movements, peering into the blackness beyond the light of his torch.

'Put up your hands, Luckman!' The clear, sharp, incisive voice of Inspector Shadgold cut the stillness like a knife.

The man's figure went suddenly rigid, and then he took a step backwards as the Scotland Yard man emerged from behind a screen of bushes, covering him with the long-barrelled automatic he held in his hand.

'Don't move!' snapped Shadgold sharply. 'You can't get away!'

Luckman glared about him like a trapped animal, as Lowe and the two plainclothes men closed in on him from behind and on either side. And then, with a snarl of rage and heedless of the detective's weapon, he sprang at Shadgold.

There was a sharp, whip-like crack as the pistol spoke, and, in the midst of his spring, Luckman seemed to crumple. He stumbled forward to his knees with a groan of pain, and then collapsed, clutching at his right ankle, the bone of which Shadgold's bullet had shattered.

'You'll have to send for a stretcher to take him away,' said Shadgold, slipping his pistol into his pocket. 'He won't be able to walk.'

'Who is it?' asked Sydney Garth, for at the appearance of Shadgold the others had hurried forward. Lowe stooped and twitched off the slouch hat the fallen man was wearing.

'Good God!' breathed Garth.

The distorted face that looked up at him was the face of Inspector Jesson!

30

Knotting the Threads

Once again the little sitting-room at Sydney Garth's cottage was full, and although the dawn was not far off, the company who had gathered there looked particularly wide awake.

After the revelation of Joseph Luckman's identity, Parrish had been sent back to Friar's Vale for a car and a stretcher, and Luckman had been safely deposited in the single cell that the little village police station boasted. Dr. McGuire had been hastily summoned to attend to the man's injured ankle, and there, closely guarded, Luckman would remain until such time as he could be transferred to the more adequate lock-up at King's Hayling, preparatory to being brought up before the magistrate and committed for trial.

The discovery that Inspector Jesson had been the man for whom they were searching was no surprise to either Lowe or Shadgold, although so far as the others were concerned it was completely unexpected. The finding of the body of the real Jesson under the heap of debris in the secret passage had completely settled any last remaining doubt that the dramatist had had. He knew that it must have been somewhere, and its discovery had formed the last link in the chain of evidence that was necessary to complete his case.

'Well, I must admit,' declared Sydney Garth, shaking his head, 'that I was astounded when I saw who it was. I never had the slightest suspicion of Jesson. What on earth was it that first turned your attention to him, Mr. Lowe?'

'Quite a simple matter,' Lowe replied. 'The Yard sent down some photographs of Luckman, among which was a very good and clear 'head and shoulders'. I got White to make some copies of this and spent the night adding the necessary trimmings to each one possessed by the people who might be Luckman. For instance, I supplied one photograph with grey hair and sketched in the characteristic lines that go to form your features, Mr. Garth. The result was nothing like you. Another I supplied with Dr. McGuire's characteristics. It was not the least like Dr. McGuire. But when I added the moustache and hair of Inspector Jesson, it was identical.

'I confirmed my suspicions, which were really more than suspicions by this time, by comparing a fingerprint of Jesson's with a fingerprint of Luckman's that we found in some paint in the lumber-room at Monk's Lodge. That settled the matter. I could have arrested him straightaway on that evidence alone, but I knew if I did that all chance of finding the diamonds was gone. There was very little hope of Luckman getting off this time on a plea of insanity, and knowing that he was going to be hanged, he would undoubtedly have kept his mouth shut regarding the whereabouts of the stones.

'I decided that the only way was to let him show us where the diamonds were hidden and then take him. I knew that there was some clue to the hiding-place in the cottage. That was obvious, and I thought that once Luckman got the impression that the place was empty, he'd immediately go there to get this clue. With this object in view, I made an announcement that I think rather astonished my young friends.' He looked across at Jack and Tony and smiled. 'I told them that I intended to return to London, and I seriously advised them to come with me. They didn't want to at first, but I eventually persuaded them. I took Shadgold into my confidence, of course, and we went down to see Inspector Jesson, to acquaint him with our decision.

'We never went further than Sunnington, and as soon as it was dusk we made our way back to Monk's Lodge and concealed ourselves in the cottage to await developments. I expected a visit that night, and I was right. Jesson arrived.

'Unfortunately for my plans, however, he managed to get away, still leaving us in the dark regarding the whereabouts of the diamonds. But at least I was pretty sure of one thing — he'd completed part of his work: he'd possessed himself of the clue which showed their hiding-place. But our interruption had effectually prevented him from making any further attempt that night to recover them. I knew that he would do so, however, at the first opportunity — probably on the following night, and I decided to take a risk. It was a big risk, but as it turned out, it was justified. I concluded that Luckman had no idea I suspected him as Jesson, and would therefore still continue to carry on with his imposture.

'Before we left King's Hayling, Shadgold had wired to the Yard asking them to send down Dickinson and Parrish, and fixing a meeting place just outside Sunnington. They arrived and were instructed to keep an eye on Jesson and trail him wherever he went. The arrangement was made regarding the confetti — and the rest you know.'

'But what a nerve the man must have had!' exclaimed Garth. 'It must have been an enormous risk to take, impersonating Jesson.'

Trevor Lowe shook his head. 'Not such a big one as you imagine. As a matter of fact, he took very little risk at all. Jesson had only recently been appointed to the position of inspector here. I learnt from the chief constable for this district that he was transferred from Minehead, which is a considerable number of miles away, and therefore knew nobody here around these parts. He took up his duties only a week before Ogden was killed, so nobody had got used to him particularly.

'Luckman possessed another advantage, which I am sure originally gave him the idea. He was almost exactly the same build as the real Jesson, and the addition of a wig and moustache made them practically identical in appearance. The only thing that might have given him away was his lack of knowledge of police routine. But here again, his difficulty wasn't so great as it might have been in a large town. The police station here is run on very rural lines. So you see, when you come to think of it, it wasn't such a terrible risk as it appears at first sight.'

'By Jove!' said Tony indignantly. 'And, if you remember, this scoundrel wanted to arrest us for the murder of Ogden!'

'Naturally,' replied Lowe. 'He wanted to kill two birds with one stone. He wanted to fix the crime on you or Jack, which would have resulted in leaving the cottage tenantless, and also stopped any further investigation into the murder. Luckman's clever — a warped cleverness, I'll admit — but still clever.'

'I don't quite see,' said Sydney Garth, 'how this change of personalities was effected. What made Luckman decide to impersonate Jesson?'

'I can only give you my theory for that.' Lowe shrugged. 'Probably it will be proved or disproved at the trial, but from what I gathered from the chief constable, I should say that it was pure accident. Apparently Jesson was at one time attached to the Metropolitan Police Force — it was at his own wish, I believe, that he be transferred to a country division — and it's my theory that at some time or other during that period he had come in contact with Luckman.

'Now, when Luckman escaped from Broadmoor every police station in the country was circularised with his description, and every police officer, from a constable upwards, was looking for him; Jesson, of course, among them. In my opinion, Jesson ran into Luckman and recognised him and was killed for his pains. Then it was, I think, that the great idea entered Luckman's brain. He was looking for somewhere near

Monk's Lodge where he could lie low, and yet be on the spot to secure the diamonds when the opportunity presented itself. And here was the very chance he wanted! Nobody would suspect for one moment that Inspector Jesson of Friar's Vale was the escaped criminal lunatic that the whole of the police force were looking for.'

'I certainly never did,' said Garth, 'although I knew that Luckman was somewhere in the neighbourhood. But why did he kill Ogden?'

'To prevent him from telling Frost that Luckman was the real owner of the cottage,' replied the dramatist. 'I think Ogden had only just learned of Luckman's escape — you know it wasn't published for some time after, and then it's doubtful if the local papers round here would have made much of a splash of it. Again I can only offer a suggestion, as the man mostly concerned is dead, and unless Luckman tells us we've no proof. In my opinion, as soon as Ogden discovered that Luckman had escaped, he came to the conclusion, on thinking it over, that it was probable he might make his way to Monk's Lodge. Like everybody else, he looked upon Luckman as a lunatic and, no doubt, thought it his duty to warn Frost that there might be danger.

'How Luckman became aware of his intention I don't know, but I should imagine the most reasonable suggestion is that Ogden either called into the police station on his way to keep the appointment, or met Luckman in his capacity of Jesson while he was walking up to Monk's Lodge. After all, it seems most natural that if Ogden had any misgivings as to the likelihood of Luckman appearing in the district, he would warn the police as well. Anyway, that's how I think it happened, and Luckman probably suggested that he should accompany him to Monk's Lodge, and at some secluded spot killed him. Of course, the reason for concealing the body in the upstairs room was to throw suspicion on the inmates.'

'What about the johnny with the beard?' asked Jack. 'How does he come into it?'

'The johnny with the beard, as you call him,' said Trevor Lowe, 'and his companion Blane were the people who helped Luckman to commit the Hatton Garden diamond robbery, and they were after the stones.

There's no doubt that Luckman double-crossed them. Murdock tells me that they knew Luckman had a place somewhere near King's Hayling, and that they always supposed that he'd hidden the diamonds there. They never believed for a moment that he'd thrown them into the Thames. Unfortunately for them, they didn't know where it was or what it was called, and for the past three years they'd been too busy dodging the police — for there's still a warrant out for their arrest over the Hatton Garden affair — to have much time to try and find it.

'When they heard that Luckman had escaped, however, they guessed that he'd make for this house of his, wherever it was, to pick up the stones, so they came down and settled in King's Hayling. They made veiled inquiries concerning any strangers who'd appeared in the neighbourhood and heard about 'Mr. Wyse's' arrival at this cottage. They instantly mistook him for Luckman, concluding that the woman who was with him was merely a blind in order to distract suspicion. Hence their unpleasant attentions.'

'And Blane?' said Garth.

'Blane found the secret passage,' answered Lowe, 'unfortunately for him. He told Murdock of his discovery and they searched the place thoroughly in the hope of discovering the diamonds. But, of course, without result. According to Murdock, however, Blane wasn't satisfied and went off on his own to have another look. He never came back. He must've chosen the time when Luckman was also prowling about in his monk's robe.'

There was a short silence which was broken eventually by Jack. 'Surely Luckman could have remembered where he'd hidden the diamonds without all this bother of drawing maps,' he remarked.

'Under the circumstances I doubt it,' said Lowe. 'As a matter of fact, he took a very sensible precaution. He knew that it was ten chances to one he would be arrested, and that possibly several years would elapse before he would be able to recover the proceeds of his crime. It is difficult to distinguish one tree from another in a forest of hundreds, and time would obliterate any mark that he might make to guide him. No,

344

the map was the only way.'

Sydney Garth looked across at a small, square, dirty iron box that stood on the table. 'They've been the cause of a number of innocent people losing their lives,' he remarked.

'They have,' agreed Trevor Lowe. 'Let's hope that their rightful owners will take care of them in future.'

He rose to his feet and, crossing to the table, picked the box up and handed it to the grey-haired man.

'Let me congratulate you,' he said, 'on having secured the feather for Thoroughgood & Co's cap!'

GRIM DEATH

MURDER IN MANUSCRIPT

THE GLASS ARROW

THE THIRD KEY

THE ROYAL FLUSH MURDERS

THE SQUEALER

MR. WHIPPLE EXPLAINS

THE SEVEN CLUES

THE CHAINED MAN

THE HOUSE OF THE GOAT

THE FOOTBALL POOL MURDERS

THE HAND OF FEAR

SORCERER'S HOUSE

THE HANGMAN

THE CON MAN

MISTER BIG

THE JOCKEY

THE SILVER HORSESHOE

THE TUDOR GARDEN MYSTERY

THE SHOW MUST GO ON

SINISTER HOUSE

THE WITCHES' MOON

ALIAS THE GHOST

THE LADY OF DOOM

THE BLACK HUNCHBACK

with Chris Verner:

THE BIG FELLOW

We do hope that you have enjoyed reading this large print book.

Did you know that all of our titles are available for purchase?

We publish a wide range of high quality large print books including:
Romances, Mysteries, Classics
General Fiction
Non Fiction and Westerns

Special interest titles available in large print are:
The Little Oxford Dictionary
Music Book, Song Book
Hymn Book, Service Book

Also available from us courtesy of Oxford University Press:
Young Readers' Dictionary
(large print edition)
Young Readers' Thesaurus
(large print edition)

For further information or a free brochure, please contact us at:
Ulverscroft Large Print Books Ltd.,
The Green, Bradgate Road, Anstey,
Leicester, LE7 7FU, England.
Tel: (00 44) **0116 236 4325**
Fax: (00 44) **0116 234 0205**

THE LADY OF DOOM

Gerald Verner

Whispers have reached Scotland Yard of an elusive figure that has appeared on the dark horizon of crime and is making its influence felt. Then the first threatening letter comes, demanding a huge payment, or death for its recipient. The victim goes to the police for protection — only to be promptly murdered. The same graft has been worked by gangsters in Chicago — and now it seems they have arrived in London. As Scotland Yard strives to find the criminal mastermind responsible, so too does a mysterious woman . . . the Lady of Doom!

RENDEZVOUS WITH A CORPSE

Fletcher Flora

The wayward beauty who comes back to her old hometown to titillate her ex-boyfriend (now a married lawyer) and to blackmail her ex-husband is ripe bait for murder. And murder is just what she gets. Suspicion falls heaviest on the old flame: he was at the scene of the crime and out of his legal mind, befuddled by a number of potent cocktails. The police find his explanation incredible; but his wife, believing in his innocence, sets out to pursue an investigation of her own . . .